FACADE

FACADE

FACADE

by Susan Cory

Facade © 2016

Published by Susan Cory

This book is a work of fiction. Names, characters, places and incidents either are products of the author's imagination or are used fictitiously. Any resemblance to actual events or locales or persons, living or dead, is entirely coincidental. All rights reserved. Except as permitted under the U.S. Copyright Act of 1976, no part of this publication may be reproduced, distributed or transmitted in any form or by any means, or stored in a database or retrieval system, without the prior written permission of the publisher.

ISBN-13: 978-0-9853702-5-1

To Dan

"He who has to be a creator always has to destroy."

Friedrich Nietzsche's *Thus spoke Zarathustra*

CHAPTER ONE

It was the irritating waft of his cigarette smoke that Iris Reid noticed first.

"I'm sorry, I didn't mean to disturb you," said a voice behind her which, yes, was disturbing her. She clapped her sketch book closed.

"I was having a coffee out here on the café terrace and I couldn't help noticing you drawing that building," the man said, delicate fingers holding the offending cigarette. "You've piqued my curiosity. Are you by chance an architectural illustrator?"

She rose to face him, her own curiosity piqued by his accent. German maybe—a bit of tonsil-clearing in those "r"s? "I'm an architect. At the moment I'm designing a townhouse to replace that Greek Revival one," she said gesturing toward a building on Mount Auburn Street near Harvard Square.

"I'm an architect too," he said and reached out a hand to shake hers.

Up close she could see that his looks were of the weather-beaten-director-at-Sundance type. He had craggy skin and wore fashionable green glasses (conspicuous eyewear being a fetish among architects), with light brown hair brushed straight back. An elegant black leather backpack was slung over one shoulder.

"Do you practice in Cambridge?" she asked. God knew, every fourth person in this town seemed to be an architect and even Iris didn't know them all.

"No, my firm is in Amsterdam. I'm here to teach for a semester at the GSD." He pronounced the initials for the Graduate School of Design "Gay Ess Day."

"Xander DeWitt," he added.

"I didn't recognize... I know your work of course... I'm Iris Reid. I'm also teaching at GSD this Fall." She moved back to look at him.

DeWitt was one of a handful of world-class architects she most respected. His office, Co-op dWa, employed 60 architects, yet he was barely forty. She'd noticed his name on the faculty roster and had been eager to meet him.

"So we'll be colleagues. Lovely." He appraised her while blowing a long stream of smoke out his nostrils. "I flew in last night and the Dean gave me a quick tour. I'm trying to get oriented.

What are you teaching?"

"Urban infill architecture, a studio for second year students. You?"

"Mine is a third year studio. Waterfront mixed use in Rotterdam."

"Are you using a project from your office?"

"Yes, we're in the middle of constructing it. The building's frame has just been completed."

Iris imagined a noisy, waterlogged building site where everything was managed with Dutch precision. Not like here. "So you'll end up taking your students to Holland? That's brave of you."

He rolled his eyes. "I'm not sure what I've gotten myself in for."

"I'm sure it will be a memorable studio." She sounded like an idiot and probably looked like a bag lady. Her long brown hair was twisted into a topknot on this sweltering early September day and she wore no make-up. Her shorts and T-shirt didn't quite match up to his linen pants and crisp white shirt. So much for first impressions.

"But I didn't mean to interrupt your sketching." He made a demurring motion with his eloquent hand. "Still I'm glad to have met a fellow professor. I'm on my way over to the Malkin Pool for a swim. I'll see you around the GSD, Iris Reid."

She stared at his back disappearing into traffic on Mount Auburn Street. So that was the legendary Xander DeWitt.

The following Friday

"It won't be that bad," Ellie assured Iris as they strolled down Oxford Street past Harvard University's Science Center. "Sure, the students will be as intense and overachieving as we were twenty years ago, but I actually enjoyed teaching the Bauhaus course last year."

The still air of summer lingered as they approached the concrete structure housing the design school.

Iris finished the last of her Vietnamese iced coffee and dumped the cardboard cup in a recycling bin near the entry. "I can't believe we agreed to do this," she groaned.

"It's not like you had much choice with the Gilles calling in his marker. And I'm doing it because I'm your saintly friend," Ellie said, looking more professional than usual with her normal explosion of red curls tamed into a neat asymmetrical bob.

"I'm forever in your debt. You're the one with the teaching experience." Iris removed her sunglasses as they entered the stuffy, badly lit Piper Auditorium.

Their long-ago professor, Gilles Broussard, was now the dean of the Architecture Department. Iris' work had popped back onto his radar at their twentieth reunion the previous June. He'd been so impressed by a house she'd designed, which had served as an informal reunion venue, that he'd championed her work to the committee searching for an architect for a townhouse for visiting GSD staff, and Iris had snagged the commission. So when a professor scheduled to teach a fall studio had dropped out at the last moment, the dean had tapped Iris to fill in.

Ellie and Iris eased into the front row with eleven other instructors, all readying their spiels so the mass of waiting students could rank their choices for the studio assignment lottery. It felt like a popularity contest. It was a popularity contest. What if no one wanted to take her course? Iris glanced around and spotted Xander DeWitt as he wended his way up the aisle. She nudged Ellie and gestured in his direction with her head.

"Mmmm," Ellie purred.

A delicate young blond man with a soul-patch and an unfortunate overbite, probably an assistant, followed in his wake. Hundreds of eyes followed DeWitt to his seat and studied him as he propped a leather briefcase, big enough to hold perhaps four sheets of paper, onto his lap. Definitely the marquee attraction.

Gilles stood at the podium fiddling with the projection remote. He tapped the mike, cleared his throat, then launched into an introduction of Professor #1, an architect from Argentina with an Einstein perm, who shuffled to the lectern. The man began to expound on studying the urban fabric from both the Latour, Sloterdijk and Habermas points of view versus a Situationist approach.

Iris' palms began to sweat. She whispered to Ellie, "Can you spout crap like that?"

"Oh yeah. We architectural historians love to talk trash."

When it was their turn, they showed PowerPoint slides of Iris' Neo-Modernist house that had caught Gilles' eye as well as other examples of buildings she had designed. The house had just been published that month in cuttingedgedecor magazine, lending them some momentary cachet. Iris stressed her experience as a practicing architect, while Ellie discussed the books she'd written and courses she'd taught.

Iris was relieved to sink back into her uncomfortable purple plastic seat and watch DeWitt drift fluidly to the podium.

As the room hushed, he clicked an image onto the screen. "I'd like to show a project that my firm has just finished constructing. It is a Jesuit Chapel in Geneva. You're seeing it 'hot off the press.'"

Iris was looking at...what? An interior shot—wavy lines embedded in warm ochre panels, juxtaposed against rough scored concrete, sometimes flat, sometimes curved.

"The panels are marble. Very thin translucent slabs used instead of glass," DeWitt explained. "The pattern from the veins forms an abstract version of stained glass. I wanted to show the passage between two worlds, the sacred and the profane, so I limited my materials to marble and concrete."

Four hundred jaws dropped quietly.

He showed more slides of this incredible building. Shapes transformed from intimate prayer rooms into a soaring nave, with plays of light masterfully orchestrated throughout.

It was utterly modern, utterly original. Iris wondered why she hadn't thought of using sliced marble this way.

An impressive cross-section of more buildings from around the globe followed. DeWitt finished up with a discussion of his studio's Rotterdam waterfront project. For the closing, he removed his glasses, and, like Clark Kent, exposed his secret weapon, a pair of striking, steel blue eyes.

As he stepped down from the podium the energy in the room

deflated. The last few speakers tried unsuccessfully to regenerate some excitement, until Gilles stepped in to wrap up the session. Students migrated out to the lobby, loudly exchanging impressions. The teaching staff, the full professors, and the actual practicing architects remained behind to socialize. Ellie was chatting with a visiting professor from her Berkeley PhD days. Iris was about to leave when Gilles appeared, Zelig-like, in her path.

"Irees, have you met Xander DeWitt yet?" The dean had left France more than twenty years before but his accent seemed to be gaining strength. "Xander, if you are teaching here two years from now, you will be able to stay in the faculty guest center Irees is designing for us."

The man of the hour's smile was sphinxlike. "We've already met. You look different today."

Iris had armored herself in "archigear" for the occasion: a gray Issey Miyake dress that draped so artfully that no one else at Filene's Basement had been able to figure out what to do with it. "You caught me off duty the other day." Was she blushing? "How have you been enjoying Cambridge?"

"It is an adorable town—almost European, and I've discovered an excellent restaurant. Maybe you'd like to join me for a meal tonight. Not that you haven't been delightful company,

Gilles."

The dean bowed his head at the compliment and took his cue to blend back into the crowd vibrating around them like a beehive. Iris felt, rather than saw, the respectful space the crowd had left around them, along with the ill-concealed sidelong glances. Xander could hardly have been as unaware of the attention as he appeared.

Iris thought about his invitation for all of a minute. Her boyfriend Luc, the owner and chef of the Paradise Café, always ran the kitchen on Friday and Saturday nights. What harm could come from an innocent dinner with a new colleague?

CHAPTER TWO

"Good evening Professor DeWitt. Let me show you to your table." The maitre d' nodded at Iris.

The Harvest had been a Cambridge institution since 1975, but Iris hadn't eaten there in ages. Located down an alley in Harvard Square, the restaurant's chef gave Luc some serious competition.

On their way to the softly lit back room, Iris and Xander passed two incongruous TVs over the bar, one set to a Red Sox game, the other to CNN. Their waitress handed them menus and walked them through the elaborate specials: wild-caught, Sumac-spiced salmon and a beet salad featuring nasturtiums "grown on their own roof garden."

Iris leaned across to Xander. "I thought Sumac was poisonous."

He smiled. "Have no fear. This berry is actually a cousin of the poisonous one. I've had it here and survived."

"How many times have you eaten here?" she asked.

"I researched the restaurant scene when I first arrived. The restaurants in Cambridge are actually better than most of the Boston ones. Half a dozen places have first-class cuisine. I was going to work my way through those six but on the third night, the combination of a talented chef and the lacquered aubergine walls here won me over so I decided to make this my local spot." He gestured to the walls. "How do you call that color in English—eggplant? So sophisticated."

Iris wondered if the Paradise Café had made Xander's list. She should find a way to mention Luc. Across the brilliant white linen, lit by candles, Xander looked quite handsome.

She broke off a chunk of corn bread. "Does your assistant join you for dinners?"

"No—that would feel too much like a continuation of work. We both prefer our privacy after hours. Nils is here as my teaching helper but he'll also fly back and forth to Amsterdam to bring me important work from the office. This weekend he's helping me get my house here organized. My plan is to come here most nights to have a lovely meal, then to return home to read, write, or listen to music."

The purity of his ritual struck Iris. What a noble way to lead your life—paring things to only the high points. She should live like this.

"What do you write about?" She kept her voice light, trying not to sound too nosy.

"Whatever speaks to me that day. Sometimes it's abstract, sometimes it's visual or relating to the senses. It depends." Xander looked around the room. "But I'm talking too much about myself. Let's order some wine, then I want to hear about you."

An attentive somelier, hovering nearby, whisked over and took Iris' order. She chose an Oregon Pinot Noir from a well-curated wine list. Iris' father had taught her a lot about wine before his untimely death so she felt confident in her choice.

"Shall I bring you a glass of the Meursault, Professor?" the sommelier asked Xander.

He gave a slight nod.

He leaned back in his chair to study her. "So what is your philosophy on life, Iris?"

The question struck Iris as so European. "I try to balance my work and my personal life," she improvised.

"Are they actually separate? Or can they be viewed on a

larger continuum. Nietzsche talks about each person becoming a poet of his own life."

Iris kept his gaze, tilting her head just a bit.

When she didn't respond, Xander went on. "You know Friedrich Nietzsche—yes? To do everything in a conscious way— whether it is eating a meal, choosing one's clothes, or teaching students. Any action can be molded into a thing of beauty. But to do so, I believe, one must develop a deeper understanding of the nature of art."

He looked away from Iris' gaze, seemingly self-conscious. "This is the nonsense I busy myself with in my writing. Most people consider it self-indulgent."

"It's not self-indulgent," Iris countered. "I was a sculpture major in college and spent most of those years obsessing about what art really is."

"Aha—I thought you might be an artist," Xander said, delighted.

"I don't think of myself as an artist now. I didn't continue making sculptures."

"Why not?"

"It was all-consuming. I didn't think I could do both— practice architecture and create worthy sculpture at the same time.

Architecture seemed more practical. Besides, my pieces were big and I would've needed a big studio."

Xander reached across the table and took her hands in his. He looked into her eyes intently. "Did you feel passionate about your sculpture?"

Iris was startled by Xander's unexpected touch, but she nodded, then smiled wistfully as she remembered her time in Roger's Garage, the sculpture studio at Dartmouth. She had practically lived in that ratty building during her last two years of college. Nothing in her life up until that point had been as satisfying as the act of carving abstract, organic creations out of thick, glued-together planks of mahogany or, when she was lucky, black walnut.

Xander gave a small tug on her hands before releasing them. "I believe we should embrace all of our passions. Most people waste time on distractions," said with complete disdain. "If you eliminate distractions, you have time for all the things that bring you joy."

Iris was suddenly conscious that the neighboring diners had become quiet and were eying them curiously. She felt relieved when the waitress arrived and slid a plate of braised pork shoulder in front of her. The scent of the rich stock mingling with the sweet aroma of cinnamon sprinkled apples made her ravenous.

After her second mouthful Iris said "I wish I could eat like this every night."

"Why can't you?" Xander asked with an arched eyebrow.

"Good question," she said. I am dating a chef after all.

Midway through the meal, Iris saw the sommelier pass by. She was about to suggest a second glass of wine when she noticed that Xander had been pacing drinking his single glass in perfect pace with his meal. This must be part of his interpretation of doing everything in a conscious way—one perfect drink to go with one perfect dinner. Iris finished her water and a busboy materialized to refill her glass.

Later, over strong espressos at their neatly-cleared table, Iris and Xander talked about their architectural projects. He asked her a lot of questions about her townhouse design and they discussed the properties of a new type of glass that Iris was considering using.

As she was about to ask him about his Rotterdam project, a short Classical melody emmanated from his inside jacket pocket, muffled by high-ply cashmere. He slipped a cell phone from his pocket, read the screen, and frowned.

"Sorry, I need to take this. I'll be right back." He raised a finger and headed toward the door.

Iris watched through the windows as he hunched over his phone, a hand over one ear.

A minute later he hurried back to the table. "That was someone from my home security service. There's been a break-in. I'm afraid I need to go." He signaled to the waiter, making a scribbling motion in the air.

"I can drive you. It'll be faster. You walked—right?"

They found her Jeep parked on Brattle Street and Xander directed her the dozen short blocks to the small Victorian house that Harvard had rented for him. Fiddling with his watchband throughout the nine minute ride, he leapt out before Iris had come to a complete stop.

The blinding blue strobe of a Cambridge Police patrol car lit up the flanks of a double-parked van from Safety First Security and a Harvard campus police car. Light from the front hall spilled out the gaping front door.

After a few words with the policeman, Xander strode quickly back to the Jeep, his face misted with sweat. He leaned through the open car window. "I'm so sorry that our evening has ended this way, Iris. We will have to have a —what do they call it—a do-over dinner. I had a delightful time. Thank you for the ride."

Then he retreated to the porch. But Iris didn't leave right away. She parked down the block and walked back. She approached the front yard, trying to make out voices over a squawking police radio. She saw Xander talking with men in three different uniforms.

"No sign of a break-in," the man in a Safety First Security uniform announced. "Don't know why the alarm went off."

"Probably a short in the system. We opened the front door ourselves with our passkey," the Harvard campus policeman said.

"Can you take a look around inside and tell us if anything's missing?" the police officer asked Xander.

As the men headed inside, Iris peeked through the windows, at a living room where nothing seemed out of place.

It struck her as ironic that an evening spent discussing life as a testament to beauty and order should end on such a chaotic note.

CHAPTER THREE

On Saturday morning at around nine, Xander, in his black silk dressing gown, carried a delicate espresso cup and saucer into the study. He consulted his watch and since he had several hours before he and Nils were planning to unpack the rest of his boxes upstairs, he decided to Skype one of his project architects who always spent Saturday afternoons at his desk in the Amsterdam office.

After logging on, he noticed an unfamiliar icon among the others. Curious, he clicked on it. It opened to reveal a disturbing image.

Two young girls playing in the woods were—oh, God, what were they doing? Or rather, what was being done to them?

As realization dawned, he dragged it to the trash, emptied the trash, then pressed the power button, waiting until the screen faded to black before he let out his breath.

Xander ran his hands through his long, wavy hair. How did this get on his laptop, and more worrisome, how had someone, presumably, learned his personal password?

He breathed deeply, allowing the galloping pace of his heart to slow down. He could conjure up plenty of people who didn't like him—competing architects, women he might have treated as afterthoughts...But this level of invasion? Someone had managed to penetrate all of the security firewalls Nils had carefully erected.

That person was taunting him, knowing he would never go to the police. But why?

Xander reached for the pack of Black Sobranies on his desk and tapped one out. His hand shook as he thumbed his Dunhill lighter and lit it.

The doorbell's jangling ring made him drop the cigarette. He quickly retrieved it, then snapped shut the laptop. Tightening his bathrobe around him, he headed for the front hall.

Could some anti-porn SWAT team have tracked the download and be encircling his house already?

Xander's shoulders lowered an inch when he recognized his neighbor through the front door glass panel. Gilles, the dean, had brought him to meet this Stuart-or-Steven-something when Gilles had showed Xander his lodgings for the semester. Xander took a second to compose his face into a friendly expression.

"Hi there. It's Stuart Kunstler from next door," the pale, freckled man with an overly large head said. "We met the other day. Sorry to call so early on a Saturday." Stuart was as unlikely a SWAT team ninja as was possible to conjure up.

Xander ushered him in to the hall. "Good morning, Stuart. Can I offer you some coffee?" Xander hoped the other man didn't notice his slight tremble when they shook hands.

"No, no, don't bother yourself. As I mentioned on Wednesday, I'll be leaving next week to go on sabbatical in Turkey. Since you'd said you didn't have a car, I thought I'd leave you the keys to my van in case you wanted to make a grocery run." Stuart held up a keyring with a small plastic dog attached. "This key unlocks the garage. The van's a stick shift. You know how to drive that, right?"

Xander was itching to get rid of this man, so he quickly agreed, "Of course. That's so kind of you to share your car. I hope you have a productive fall in Turkey—Istanbul if I remember correctly. It's a fascinating city."

Stuart finally took his leave and Xander promptly dumped the keys into a kitchen drawer with no intention of ever using them. He found his iPhone on the kitchen table, checked the time, then tapped the first entry on his speed dial.

"Nils? Can you swing by my place? I need your help."

Nils responded, "I was planning to come by in an hour to help you unpack the boxes."

"It's about something else, an emergency."

"Fine. I'll ride over now."

Nils would know how to make sure all signs of the incriminating pornography were truly erased. Hopefully it hadn't yet shown up on the radar of anyone official tasked with monitoring who downloaded this kind of stuff.

As Xander lit a new cigarette and sucked in another hit of nicotine, an idea occurred to him. Maybe this had something to do with the previous night's break-in. Maybe the point of it had not been to take something away, but rather to leave something behind.

CHAPTER FOUR

"How did it go? What did you talk about? I want to hear everything." Ellie's voice preceeded her as she entered Iris' kitchen at noon on Saturday. "I can't believe you went to dinner with Mr. Hot-Stuff last night and didn't even call me afterward to tell me all the details."

"I'm telling you now."

Ellie made a beeline for the two signature sandwiches from Darwin's laid out on the counter and after examining both, claimed the roast beef, and grabbed a stool.

"The guy is amazing," Iris gushed. "He's orchestrated his whole life perfectly. He's not just obsessed with creating great buildings. He writes poetry, for God's sake! Everything he eats and drinks is carefully chosen. He swims every morning before work. From the three outfits I've seen him wear, he wears only shades, no colors."

"Sounds exhausting," Ellie said as she eliminated the radish sprouts from her sandwich.

Iris forked her unwanted pickle onto Ellie's plate. "By the way, the pork shoulder at the Harvest is incredible. I highly recommend it."

"What did you talk about? Weren't you intimidated?"

"He asked me about my philosophy of life and what I was passionate about."

"Whoa, what a come-on line!" Ellie said.

Iris chewed thoughtfully. "But it wasn't. There was no sexual vibe. He's just one of those rare people who is turned on by his life's work. I wish I could be more like him. I like my profession, but it's not consuming the way it is with him. I waste so much of my time on junk. Junk food, junk TV, junk reading. Maybe if I were more self-disciplined I would be designing the world's best architecture like him."

Ellie cupped her hand to her ear. "Is this *cuttingedgedecor*'s September centerfold I'm hearing?"

"I'm small potatoes compared to him. Damn, do you think it's too late to reboot my career?"

"He may have designed some incredible buildings, but as far as creating a perfect life, let's get real. The guy's in his forties, has never been married, doesn't have kids, and doesn't seem to have a serious 'other,' either female or whatever. That's not my idea of a life of beauty and balance. At the end of the day, all he has is his work."

"Yeah, I was wondering about that too. I've never heard any gossip about his social life. I was prepped with my speech about already being in a relationship, but he never showed any romantic interest in me."

"Then why do you think he was so intent on taking you out to dinner?"

"Maybe he just wanted company. He seemed interested in my life, which was flattering and surprising. He encouraged me to go back to making sculptures."

"With all your spare time?"

"If I did away with distractions the way he has I'd have enough time."

"Distractions? Like me and Luc?"

"Of course not. You know what I'm talking about."

Ellie held up a funnel next to some bottles in the island sink. "What's going on with these?"

"I'm pouring shampoo and conditioner into glass bottles. It drives me crazy that products for women only come in insipid pink or mauve plastic. Do these companies think we're Barbie dolls?"

Ellie shook her head slowly. "This is a slippery slope, my friend. You're picking up his obsessiveness. What's next—eating only white food? Tell me what happened at the end of the evening. Did he give you a peck on the cheek?"

"I almost forgot that part. As we were finishing our coffee, he got a call from his alarm service about a break-in, so we rushed over to his house."

"You're kidding! Did they catch anybody?"

"No, it must have been a false alarm—maybe a short circuit in the wiring. Nothing even looked disturbed."

"Maybe another starchitect wanted to steal one of his designs."

"I wouldn't mind stealing one of his designs," Iris admitted.

Ellie's eyes drifted down to Sheba, Iris' six-year-old basset hound, who was parked at her feet and giving Ellie her most pathetic look. "She never feeds you, does she?" Ellie said, passing down a crust.

Iris looked affectionately at her chubby dog and tsked tsked. "You're a complete fraud."

Sheba's overly-short legs combined with her overly-long ears gave her a comical appearance. The hound's expression could morph from dignified to groveling in the seconds it took the scent of beef drippings to waft to her sensitive nose.

After feeding Sheba another crust, Ellie continued, "I'll make you a bet. If you ever dropped in on Demigod DeWitt unexpectedly some evening, I'll bet you'd see him eating Doritos in his jammies and watching sitcoms, not reading Schopenhauer."

Iris shook her head. "You cynic. Here's the rare guy who's devoted his whole life to one thing—the creation of beauty."

CHAPTER FIVE

The following Monday, Iris and Ellie gathered with their students in a meeting alcove on the third level. The four floors of studios resembled a giant row of bleachers with four enormous steps. The vast, open interior housed up to six hundred students who worked on one of the giant steps under a sloping glass roof which leaked frequently—usually when final drawings had been laid out on desks waiting for a presentation. To Iris, the space seemed antiseptic at this early point in the year, since the smells of stale coffee and unwashed students had yet to build up. That sensory load would begin to ramp up as soon as the first studio deadline approached.

Iris gave silent thanks to Professor Ito who'd cancelled for leaving her with a second year studio to teach. Her ten students had none of the frozen-in-the-headlights look of first years or the brittle, embattled look of third years. Not to mention Harvard's burned-out, extra-semester students who were rarely seen. The ten in front of her looked relaxed and eager to dive into the intellectual pursuits of a new semester. The class composition was a mix, equal males to females. Half of them were international students.

Ellie began: "Why don't you each tell us a little about yourselves and how you spent the summer?"

Predictably, many had worked as underpaid interns, slaving over 3-D models, fetching coffee, or sorting carpet samples in architectural offices around the country. Most seemed to enjoy an easy camraderie developed over the previous school year spent in intense proximity. Not all, though. Iris studied the two who didn't seem to fit the mold.

Rory was in a different movie from his classmates. Contrasting with their plaid shirts and jeans, was his well-cut sport jacket with a monogramed shirt. His aquiline nose and posh British accent suggested he was just stopping by after a weekend house party at his country estate. But despite the elitist vibe, he seemed genial and his classmates appeared to accept him as an eccentric, but welcome, member of the pack. Rory had spent the summer in London working in "Uncle Marty's" London office. Someone helpfully explained to Iris and Ellie that "Uncle Marty" was Sir Martin Alsop, who'd won a Pritzker Prize for designs such as the Freerly House Museum and the Queen's Dome in London. The

Pritzker was an architect's version of an Oscar, except only one was awarded each year.

Another student leaned against a nearby wall as if using it to prop herself up. Jasna, a tall impossibly thin woman, dressed in baggy harem pants and a black top cinched with a belt, seemed shrouded in isolation. She watched the others with large soulful eyes behind wire-rim glasses. When it was her turn to speak, her softly accented words required everyone to lean in toward her. She had spent the summer in New Hampshire working as a carpenter for a contractor. Name, rank and serial number—no elaboration. Iris felt the others regard Jasna warily as if she were an volatile organic compound.

Ellie passed around printed syllabi for the course. "This studio is meant to be an in-depth study of the urban infill project that Iris is actually working on now. The schedule of pin-ups and reviews is listed. I'll be starting off our studio times with short presentations on topics such as the history of townhouses, public versus private spaces, and the interrelatedness of interior and exterior. Today Iris will give you the project brief including all the necessary spaces and technical requirements. Following that, we'll take a walk over to visit the site on the other side of Harvard Square."

While most of the students were jotting down notes on the hand-outs, Jasna had dropped into a chair and crossed her arms, not bothering to record anything.

Iris described the project itself—a townhouse with private and communal spaces for six visiting GSD professors. She explained the site requirements and concluded with "this studio will be exploring designing in cross section as well as plan. We'll look at using new materials. We'll even design a structural system. By the end of this semester you'll have experience putting a building together from start to finish. We'll progress from diagrams, to clay or cardboard massing models, to digital models using Rhino software, ending up with a full set of drawings and a detailed physical model."

Rory steepled his manicured hands and asked, "Would you mind if I hand-drafted my final work? I find the quality of the drawings to be richer."

"By all means do it by hand," Iris said. "In fact, you might even get extra credit for hand-drafting." Big smile. She herself disliked the rigidity of computer-aided design. She looked around for more questions but ten expressions telegraphed "got it."

After Ellie and Iris' introductory presentation, the students retreated to their nearby desks to lock up their laptops and grab their cameras for the field trip. Most workspaces were paired off in tight, two-person pens, with partners in the confined areas referred to as "butt-mates." Iris looked to see who Jasna's butt-mate was but the desk next to hers was empty. A lone luxo lamp and backpack occupied her space.

Iris wondered if, like herself twenty years before, Jasna had a voice inside her head telling her she didn't belong here.

CHAPTER SIX

That evening, Iris pressed the buzzer at Luc's condo before letting herself into the entry with a key he'd given her the month before. Why did she still buzz first? He knew she was coming over.

Sheba whined and shivered as Iris nudged her into the rickety cage elevator. "Sorry, girl. I'm too exhausted to walk up five flights."

Luc's 1930's brick condo building was located across the street from his restaurant, the Paradise Café, and just a few blocks from Iris' Victorian home-cum-office. They'd been spending most nights together when Luc wasn't cooking, but he'd gone over to his mother's house the previous evening for the family's monthly Sunday dinner, a ritual to which Iris had not yet been invited.

His door stood ajar. As Iris entered the unit, she heard him call out, "In the kitchen."

Luc was bent over the island, with a knife flashing through a yellow pepper, dicing it to bits. His blond hair fell below the collar of his black shirt and his sleeves were rolled up to reveal strong forearms that contrasted with slender, elegant hands. He was six years younger than Iris. They had been together for three months, still within the so-called "honeymoon" phase of a relationship.

He looked up as he swept the pepper into a salad bowl, gave her a slow and easy smile, then wiped his hands on his apron. "How'd your first day go?"

She walked over, raised her face to Luc's and kissed him deeply. Soon she was cocooned in his embrace, and when she spoke, it was against his hair. "It's looking up now."

After a minute he murmured, "Even better after I get you some Prosecco." He retrieved a bottle from the fridge, and soon placed a brimming flute on the pine kitchen table.

Iris sank gratefully into a chair, the woven rush creaking agreeably. The wooden salad bowl Luc had just positioned in front of her joined a warm baguette nested in a napkin-lined basket, silver candlesticks, and a vase of blood red ranunculi to create an inviting setting.

"This looks beautiful— but you shouldn't have to cook on your night off."

"We're celebrating your first day teaching. I want to hear all about it." He joined her at the table. "What are your students like?"

"Well, they didn't stalk off to Gilles' office demanding to be reassigned, so I'll take that as a sign of success."

Sheba, settled comfortably under the table, could be heard chomping on some delicacy (far better fare than the leftovers Iris usually provided) from a plate Luc had set down nearby.

The pinkish light of dusk filtered through the two walls of windows in the tall corner kitchen. Luc stuck his iPod into the stereo system's dock, and Nina Simone's throaty voice purred *I want a little sugar in my bowl.* Outside, the warm September evening settled into twilight, still sultry, even as the days were getting noticeably shorter. Fall was coming.

"I'm trying out a new recipe for scallops, *Cara.*" Luc poured himself a glass of Prosecco and lifted it. "*Salute.* To you and Ellie surviving the semester."

Iris understood most of the Italian words that Luc would often lapse into, courtesy of his seven years as chef in his own restaurant in Rome. She daydreamed about taking Italian lessons and traveling around Italy with him. But then she would stop herself. No projecting things too far into the future. After Iris' brief, unhappy marriage, and a subsequent series of loser boyfriends, she was gun shy.

Later, between bites of succulent scallops, Iris tried to

describe her students. She told Luc about the brittle young woman who held herself apart from the others, and the British student who everyone seemed to like despite his snobby, upper class trappings. She told him about her plan to show the class how to organize a project from start to finish.

"This design studio sounds pretty ambitious. Are you sure you'll have enough time for this *and* the townhouse commission?" Luc asked, leaning back in his chair, long legs stretched out in front of him.

"I'll have to make time. If I'm going to teach, I want to do it well," Iris said, a hint of challenge in her voice.

"Just seems like you're juggling two full-time jobs."

"That's why I have Ellie sharing the teaching with me."

"Uh huh," said Luc, chewing, watching Iris.

"What?"

"Nothing." Luc stared at the contents of his glass as he twirled the stem, then continued, "I was just remembering the last time I got myself overextended. It led to big problems."

Iris felt a prick of irritation. "Sometimes it feels like I fritter away too much of my life when I should be focused on more important things."

"Like work?"

"No, not just work. Things that really push me creatively, like maybe starting to build sculptures again. I've been remembering how much satisfaction I got from building up a large block of wood, then chiseling it down into an organic shape."

"Why would you want to add another activity to your plate when you're already so busy?"

"I just need to be more deliberate about what I spend my time doing. A professor I met at GSD, Xander DeWitt, said that if you love what you're doing, it's not really work. It's your life."

Luc leaned down to scratch behind Sheba's ears and said casually, "Who's Xander DeWitt?"

CHAPTER SEVEN

It had been six months since Jasna had tracked down the Bosnian grocery store in Watertown and since then she'd made it a point to stop in at least once a week. A bell tinkled as she entered and headed straight for the check-out counter. Lara was there as usual, still dressed in her Catholic school uniform, hunched over a book. Her dark brown hair curtained most of her oval face, showing just a slice of her fine features.

"Hi Lara," Jasna said. "How's the homework coming?"

Lara lifted her striking hazel eyes and smiled shyly at Jasna. "I was hoping you'd come today." She turned the book face down. "Homework's OK. We're reading *A Tree Grows in Brooklyn* in English class now. Have you read it?"

"No. Is it good?"

"Really good. Francie, the main character, is eleven when the book starts. She has to work in a factory. And later, she doesn't get to go to high school because they're poor." Lara's voice caught.

"It's really sad."

"Lara," a gruff voice boomed from the storeroom doorway. "The customers don't have time for silly talk." Her father stood, wiping his hands on his apron glaring at them both.

"I was just asking Lara if the Mjevena coffee is by the Nutella," Jasna said.

The girl came out from behind the counter to lead Jasna to a section of shelves between the pungent spices and the jars of jam. Jasna watched the father retreat back to the storeroom.

Lara was all long legs and thin arms, like a young Jasna at age twelve. Jasna tried discretely to spot bruises like the one she'd caught sight of a week before when Lara's long sleeves had ridden up her arm, but Lara didn't reach far for anything this time. Jasna quietly clenched her fists.

The father had a disturbing resemblance to a German hedgehog doll she'd seen once in a shop window in Montreal, soon after she'd moved there with her brother. This guy had the same fuzzy bristles on his head and same ugly stub nose.

Lara handed Jasna the bag of coffee. "Go on. Smell it."

This had become their ritual. Jasna had told Lara that just one sniff could transport her across the ocean back to Bosnia. Jasna had been only thirteen when she'd left her homeland, too young to care for coffee, but its rich comforting small carried her back to that shabby kitchen in Srebrenica which had once been the center of her world. Not that she'd ever want to actually make that trip.

Lara giggled as Jasna sniffed then went into a fake swoon. She said, "How about some cevapi for your dinner? I made it this morning before school and it's really good."

Jasna smiled. "I thought I recognized that amazing aroma." They headed over to the steam table and Jasna lifted the lid from a stainless steel pan. "Mmm, I'll take three of these. You're quite the saleswoman."

Lara scooped three of the minced lamb and beef kabobs into a waxed paper carton and Jasna added it to her basket.

As she passed the bakery section she said, "I had better get some Somun bread to go with the kababs. And maybe some of this Travnički cheese." She filled up her basket and brought it to the check-out counter.

The creak of the heavy storeroom door opening again caused them both to stiffen. In her peripheral vision, Jasna could see the father standing immobile, arms crossed, watching them.

After Lara slid her change across the counter, Jasna gave the girl a quick smile, then hurried out of the store with her plastic bag. Her mouth was dry, and her body was damp with sweat. She unlocked her bike, got on a bit unsteadily, and edged out into traffic.

She had to do something about this situation. Had Lara's father seen the girl slip the note into Jasna's bag of groceries?

CHAPTER EIGHT

The following Monday afternoon the heat wave broke and an impossibly blue sky crystallized beyond the GSD's glass roof. Terrace doors were propped open at the ends of the stepping studio levels to let in the crisp breezes of a New England fall.

Iris was working her way through one-on-one desk crits, or informal working sessions with her five students to review their initial design strategies. Five foot high, gray Homasote walls surrounded each workspace, creating individual fortresses. Iris, perched on a backless stool in Jasna's pod, huddled over an array of sketches on yellow tracing paper. In just one week Jasna had come up with some interesting concepts. The fragile young woman, dressed in an army jacket and lace-up boots, explained her theory that the urban context on busy Mount Auburn Street made privacy a priority. She pointed out that the site was crowded by other large buildings, cutting off light and air. In response, she had oriented her building inward, toward a multilevel courtyard.

Iris had removed her laptop from a tote and was searching for images to show Jasna of a similar courtyard townhouse in a dense suburb of Tokyo when she noticed Xander, in a pressed navy shirt and perfectly matching pants, standing in the opening to the pod.

"So sorry to disturb you both. May I borrow you for a moment, Iris?" he asked.

Iris followed him out of the studio into the dimly-lit corridor, where he gave her a sheepish look.

"I'd like to apologize again for how our dinner ended last week. I was having such a good time talking with you. On Saturday I'm going up to Manchester, New Hampshire to visit a Frank Lloyd Wright house. Would you be interested in joining me on this small pilgrimage? We could have lunch somewhere and make it a day." He waited expectantly.

Iris' mind froze. Viewing a building by one architectural celebrity while in the company of another was wildly tempting. But she and Luc had plans to go apple-picking on Boston's North Shore on Saturday. She couldn't cancel on him to go off with another guy, could she? No.

"I'm afraid I already have plans for Saturday."

"I understand, of course. Sorry to pull you out of class. We

46

must have a do-over dinner. I insist." Xander ducked in to give her a light kiss on each cheek, turned smoothly, and headed toward his office.

She wandered back to Jasna's pod and found her student tapping away on Iris' laptop. Had she left the thing turned on with her password entered and everything?

Jasna looked up and smiled. "I hope you don't mind. I found the photos of the Japanese courtyard building you were looking for."

Iris tried to refocus her attention on Jasna's project but her mind kept trying to parse the meaning of Xander's invitation. Maybe it was time to mention to him that she had a boyfriend.

CHAPTER NINE

Jasna squinted into the afternoon sun as she waited on the stoop of the tired old apartment building where she'd lived for the last year and a half. When she saw the slight form of the cyclist approaching, she stood up and waved.

Twenty minutes later, in the safety of her kitchen, Jasna poured fragrant orange tea from a copper pot into a pair of small ceramic cups. Lara perched on her chair, silent.

Jasna looked at the girl encouragingly. "You said you needed to ask me something?"

The girl stared into her tea cup as she spoke. "Tata's mad that I won't wear a hijab to school. He says I have to honor my heritage."

Jasna stirred some honey into her tea then asked, "Why don't you want to wear one?"

Lara looked at her wide-eyed. "Are you kidding? And be pointed out as 'the Arab kid'? Sure, my school has other non-

Catholic students, but I don't want everyone to look at me like a weirdo." Lara looked down at the floor. "But there's something worse. Now he's saying he's going to send me back to Bosnia this summer, after I turn thirteen, to marry some guy from his village—a guy as old as him."Jasna slid her chair closer. "Damn," she said under her breath.

Tears leaked from Lara's eyes. "Do you believe it? He said that's the only way I can stay unsullied. He said that was how old my mother was when they married."

The girl looked at Jasna with desperation. "I have to run away. I can cook. I'll go to California and he'll never find me. But I need some money. If you could lend me something to take the bus to California I would pay you back when I get a job as a cook. I promise I'll send you the money."

Jasna covered Lara's hands with her fingers. "We'll figure something out."

"Tata says he'll kill me if I tell anyone about this. It will disgrace the family. I'm supposed to follow the path that Allah set out for women. But I'll kill myself if he makes me do this!"

"No you won't. Let me ask you, if you did disappear, how hard would he look for you?"

"Very hard. The man in Bosnia is going to give him a lot of

money for me. Tata says I must repay him for feeding me and giving me a place to live. He has lots of friends in Watertown and they would help him hunt me down. That's why I have to go to California. I need to be far away."

Jasna nodded. "Would he go to the police to tell them you're missing?"

"I don't know. He doesn't trust the police." Lara rubbed her finger along the scarred edge of the wooden table. "He might, though." She looked past Jasna to the microwave's clock and rose. "I should go. I skipped chess club and he'll be expecting me."

Jasna rested a hand on Lara's shoulder. "Hang on. Let me think about this for a minute." She got up and stared out the window at nothing. She thought about the plans she'd been making for the last six months and how this development would complicate everything.

After fifteen minutes Jasna returned to the table, far calmer than she had any reason to be. "I will help you Lara, but I need to explain something to you first."

CHAPTER TEN

Why hadn't she started this sooner? Iris thought as she stomped up the open steel stairway to the fourth level. It was the last Friday in September and her interim student evaluations were due today, but she couldn't get the GSD website to accept her password. Even web-savvy Ellie hadn't been able to figure out what the problem was. So now she needed to take a break in the middle of Studio to throw herself on the mercy of Peg, Gilles' assistant, who would undoubtedly scold her for leaving things to the last minute.

Peg was a woman of advanced years, with a head of improbably red hair. She sat at her desk in the reception area outside Gilles' office and controlled access to her boss with fierce loyalty. She peered at her computer screen through her thick eyeglasses before finally looking up.

"Professor Reid, I noticed that you haven't submitted your student forms yet." The faint accusation was delivered in a nasal midwestern accent.

Iris explained her dilemma, then watched Peg's computer screen over the older woman's shoulder as she tried to trouble-shoot the problem. This gave Iris a close-up view of the gray roots on the back of Peg's scalp, no doubt overlooked during a home dye job.

Peg instructed Iris to type in her password, and looked away while Iris carefully did so. The "password incorrect" message shot back.

"Are you sure you're remembering your password correctly? Did you write it down anywhere?"

"Of course I remember it. I always use the same one."

Peg gave her an appalled look. "That's how people get their identities stolen." She glanced down at a metal corner peeking out of Iris' tote bag. "Good, you brought your laptop. Sit here and open up your e-mail so you can get a new password."

Iris opened her e-mail account, retrieved a change-password message page and cast her eyes to the ceiling, trying to think of a word she would be likely to remember, other than 'Sheba1,' her usual one. When prompted she typed in "Luccormier."

At the sound of a light tap-tap on the doorframe, both women looked up. A preteen girl in a plaid school uniform appeared in the doorway. She had black-fringed hazel eyes, innocently beautiful.

Peg looked up, focused on the girl, and asked "May I help you, dear?"

"I'm looking for Professor DeWitt's office." The girl's voice was soft and she seemed nervous.

Peg pointed. "It's number 414, about eight doors down on your right."

As the door swung shut again, they could hear light footsteps recede down the hallway.

Iris hit a button on her keyboard, and her student evaluation page emerged on the screen.

CHAPTER ELEVEN

Sheba's stubby Bassett Hound leg waggled in time to Iris' rhythmic belly patting as they sprawled together on the leather Corbusier sofa in Iris' living room.

"Uh, oh. This poor guy's in trouble, Sheba. The next clue says he has to find unpasteurized cheese in the middle of Detroit. I can't watch." But Iris' eyes remained glued to the TV. Sure enough, the latest *Urban Survivor*-hopeful, a software salesman from New Mexico, could be seen racing wild-eyed through the Motor City's mean streets, fruitlessly confronting people for the location of a gourmet grocery. Meanwhile, his opponent, a blackjack dealer from New Jersey with the improbable name of Shelli, was trying to track down a Vietnamese pot-bellied pig in the middle of St. Louis, a far harder task in Iris' estimation. It would be one thing if they were allowed to have their smart phones. Back in the studio, the show's hosts made snarky comments about the contestants' progress while the studio audience shouted out encouragement for their favorite player.

But the spell of the show was broken when a commercial for Fluffy's Fiesta cat food came on and Sheba lifted her head suspiciously from the sofa. When a clowder of cats started mewing on screen, Sheba growled deep in her throat.

Why am I watching this? Iris clicked off the remote. "That does it, Sheba. No more junk TV."

It had been a month since she'd first met Xander DeWitt, and one dinner and two lunches later her respect for the man had not diminished. At their last lunch at the Harvard Faculty Club he had almost convinced her to create a sculpture studio in her basement with all the heavy tools and equipment that would entail.

Iris looked at her watch—a black-faced Movado with no numbers that had been her father's. Eight-forty-five. Her brain was too tired to work on the townhouse design. She should get some exercise.

"Walkies, Sheebz."

The dog regarded her mistress with puzzlement. This was not the usual drill.

"I'm serious. COME."

Sheba trudged after her to the kitchen and allowed her leash to be snapped on, her Ringo Starr eyes telegraphing serious disapproval.

As Iris opened her kitchen door a cool October breeze hit her. She turned back to grab a suede jacket from the front hall closet, and they headed up Washington Avenue, passing Victorian houses, lit up to expose doll-house-like vignettes of the life within. Iris felt virtuous, strolling purposefully in the chilly air. Her neighborhood was still fairly safe to walk around at night, especially for someone with a brown belt in karate.

As they approached Mass Ave, the long, meandering spine of Cambridge, Iris looked to her left, toward the Paradise café where Luc was busy cooking tonight. Sheba started to head in that direction, but Iris tugged her to the right instead. They passed Judy Jetson's Hair Salon where only a month before Judy herself had given Ellie her new hairdo. They passed one-off storefronts, here today, gone after Christmas, that gave the neighborhood a faint bohemian charm. Further along, music and raucous voices spilled out from a recessed doorway, along with several wobbly customers from the Temple Bar's sleek facade.

At a red light in front of Starbucks, Iris told Sheba, "*This* is our new nightly routine."

They continued past some Harvard Law School dorms, rounded a corner, and reached the construction site for yet another new Harvard Bioscience building. She'd been wanting to check the progress of this new addition to the campus, but the lack of any street lights left the building's skeleton looking like an undefined lump under its tarps billowing in the darkness.

Oh, honestly. Harvard's endowment is the largest in the world and they can't afford to light up their buildings at night?

The silence seemed unnatural in this deserted block. Looking off to the sides, Iris picked up her pace, wrapping her jacket more tightly around her, until she found herself and Sheba traversing the two short blocks toward Howland Street.

Xander's street.

Had this been her real destination? Had thinking about the man earlier, about his compelling example of a life well lived, drawn her half-consciously to his house? Was it curiosity that had led her here as if pulled by a force field? Now that she was here, the ridiculousness of her trajectory sank in. She couldn't just ring his doorbell at nine o'clock at night. What did she even want from this man?

Beyond the porch she could see a sliver of light escaping from between the curtains of the bay window, so he was probably home. Maybe he had company.

She *had* been meaning to ask him the name of a self-cleaning glass product that he'd mentioned at their last lunch. Oh, who was she kidding? She could ask him that in an e-mail.

The night of the break-in was the only time she'd been to his house before. Maybe the fact that she had turned down his invitation to the New Hampshire excursion had dampened his interest in her.

At this point, as Iris stood in his front yard mesmerized by the light from his living room, her curiosity about what Xander was doing was gaining strength. She found herself drifting up the porch stairs and over to the brightly lit window, tugging Sheba behind her.

At first she thought she saw an empty room. Then she noticed Xander sitting on the floor, not eight feet away. Luckily, he was facing sideways with his eyes closed. He wore black pajamas— silk from their sheen. He had a pair of earphones clamped on. Resting his back against the sofa, he had an ecstatic look on his face, his left hand gently stroking a throw pillow.

Iris watched in fascination. She squinted to read the title on the CD jewel case but his hand covered the writing. She could almost hear the romantic music that must be producing the look on Xander's face—Debussy, or maybe Grieg, something like that.

Across the room two of Arne Jacobsen's classic Swan chairs

faced the understated greige sofa. Nestled in the crossed feet of one chair was a bottle of some amber liquid, its label facing away. As Iris looked closer, she spotted an empty shot glass in Xander's idle right hand. He must have saved his nightly alottment of alcohol for savoring after dinner.

Ellie had called what Iris felt for Xander a "professional crush," but maybe it was his entire lifestyle she coveted, not just the professional part. She wanted to live like him, have his career, but still surround herself with her friends. Was that too much to ask?

Sheba took this moment to let out an impatient whine. Iris froze as Xander's eyes opened and he cocked his head toward the window.

Then she flew down the porch steps, dragging Sheba behind her.

CHAPTER TWELVE

It was Friday, the second day in a row that Jasna hadn't been in class. Iris had instructed her students to e-mail her if they were sick or had to miss Studio for any reason, but Jasna had maintained radio silence. When Iris grilled her students, Rory mentioned that Jasna had borrowed his car two nights before, but had returned it to its parking spot the next morning. That was the last time anyone had seen or heard from her.

In Iris' vivid imagination, Jasna lay on the floor of her apartment, deathly ill, struggling to reach for her cell phone. The thought propelled her down the hall toward the dean's office and Peg, the keeper of everyone's contact information.

But as she entered the fourth floor office, Peg's eyes lit up and she waved a folded newspaper in Iris' direction. "Professor Reid—I was just going to call you! Have you seen the *Globe* today? It's that young girl who asked us for directions."

Iris took the paper Peg handed her and laid it flat on the desk. On the bottom of the front page ran a headline: **Cambridge Girl Missing** above a close-cropped photo of the girl who had come to this office the previous week looking for Xander. Iris looked carefully. It was definitely the same girl.

"I think I should call the police to tell them about her visit," Peg said, "but I don't want to get Professor DeWitt in trouble."

Iris held up one finger and eased into the visitor's chair to scan the whole article.

Lara Kurjak, twelve, is a seventh grader at St. Peter's School in Cambridge. Her father, Ivano, returned from his weekly card game on Wednesday night to find her missing from their apartment. There was no sign of a break-in. She is described by her father and teachers as a sweet, quiet girl. Anyone with information about her whereabouts is asked to call the police hotline: 617-555-3300.

Iris noted the byline: Robert Buchanan Jr.—or "Budge" as he'd been known to her Dartmouth class twenty-some years before, for no reason that Iris could remember. She shuddered. She could still picture Budge and his snickering cronies lying in wait at Thayer Dining Hall, holding up written numbers from one to ten to rank the looks of any co-ed who walked past their table.

Peg's voice brought her back to the present. "What should we do?"

"When did we see her?"

"Friday. Remember—the student evaluations were due."

"And from what it says here she disappeared the following Wednesday—two days ago." Wednesday. Iris felt her cheeks flush. *Wednesday night was when she had gone by Xander's house.*

She managed to say, "Professor DeWitt must have some legitimate connection to this girl but we should still call the police. They'll want to talk to anyone who knew her. Have you discussed this with Gilles?"

"No," Peg moaned. "I didn't get around to reading the paper until this afternoon. The Dean flew out to Texas for a fundraising event today."

"When is he coming back?"

"Later tomorrow. Do you think it can wait?"

"No," Iris said. "The poor girl is gone and the first days are crucial. You should call that number now."

As Peg punched the phone buttons, Iris slipped out of the room, completely forgetting to ask for Jasna's home address.

CHAPTER THIRTEEN

Sitting at Ellie's kitchen island, Iris raised her voice to be heard over the crackling of browning onions. "Have you read about the missing St. Peter's girl?"

"What?" Ellie turned off the burner and came over to look at the front page of the *Globe* that Iris had found sitting on the top of a pile in Ellie's blue recycling bin.

"Oh, yeah...that poor girl. Have the police learned anything yet?"

"No, but here's the weird thing," Iris said. "A week ago this same girl came by Peg's office when I was there and asked for directions to Xander's office."

Ellie wiped her hands on her apron. "Why would a kid be looking for Xander? He doesn't have any children."

"I have no idea. But he might have some information about her that could help the police with their search."

"He couldn't have had anything to do with taking her, could

he?"

"No, of course not! Besides, she disappeared on Wednesday night and I happened to see Xander that night."

"You mean you went out with him again? And you didn't tell me?" Ellie scrunched up her face in a mock glare.

"I didn't go out with him. I was just out walking Sheba and... I saw him."

"What do you mean you were 'just out walking Sheba'? You never walk her at night. And Xander lives on Howland Street. That's not even in our neighborhood."

Iris looked intently at the butcher block counter. "I wanted to stretch my legs and check out the construction on the new Bioscience building. Then I happened to pass his house on our way back and..."

"You peeked in his windows?" Ellie narrowed her eyes. "I can't believe you stalked him without inviting me along."

"I was NOT stalking him! You had said that thing about betting he didn't really write poetry at night but watched TV instead, so I was curious."

"Curious. And what did you see when you SPIED on him?"

"I was NOT spying. I was... I don't know what I was doing,

but I did happen to see him that night, so I know he wasn't off abducting that girl. He was sitting in his living room in his pajamas, listening to music through headphones. Looking innocent. Not watching TV and eating potato chips, by the way."

"And what time was this?"

"Around nine."

"What time did the girl go missing?"

"The paper doesn't say."

"Hmm."

"Peg called the police hotline a little while ago to tell them about the girl's visit to GSD last week. She didn't want to get Xander into any trouble, but I told her she should call them."

"Of course, she should've called them. Xander might be able to help them find the girl. And since you saw him sitting at home that night, he shouldn't get in any trouble."

"Except that for me to be Xander's alibi, I'd have to tell the world that I'd been peeking in his window."

Ellie gave her a stern look. "Then let's hope he has an innocent explanation for her visit and doesn't need you to cover for him."

*   *   *

Back at home, Iris clicked on the Six O'Clock News to see if the missing girl story was getting much play. She and Sheba leaned forward on the sofa as the familiar school photograph of Lara appeared while a distracting newsreel banner about a new financial scandal scrolled across the bottom of the screen. A newscaster made a concerned face and announced an upcoming press conference with the father of the missing Cambridge girl.

Iris got up to pour herself a glass of Pinot Noir during the commercial break and returned in time to catch a tough, angry-looking man with an incongruous upturned nose and dark stubble on his head and chin seated at a table in front of a microphone. A name plate identified him as Ivano Kurjak.

Several detectives stood behind him.

"I want Lara back," the rough-looking man said in a thick Slavic accent. "She's a good girl and I want her back safe." Then he crossed his arms and sat back in his chair. The effect was menacing, as if he was issuing an ultimatum. To reclaim the viewer's sympathy, the camera quickly panned to a blown-up photo of Lara, propped on the table next to him.

A detective spoke into another microphone, explaining that the girl had gone missing from her apartment on May Street in Cambridge some time between 7 and 9 P.M. on Wednesday, October 3rd. He urged anyone who might have seen anything at all that evening to come forward as soon as possible, to call the police hotline number which now scrolled across the bottom of the screen.

Iris was nibbling on her nails, deep in thought when her cell phone buzzed.

"Are you watching the news?" Ellie asked.

"Yeah. I saw this girl once and I'm already feeling haunted by her. Did that father seem sinister to you? The newspaper said he's a widower so he's all the girl has. Do you think he might have done something to her?"

"He seems like the type with a short fuse. Maybe he drinks and gets violent or something."

"I hope she's just run away." Iris said.

"At least there was no mention of any Harvard professors, so maybe you can keep your secret about stalking Xander."

CHAPTER FOURTEEN

*F*amous Harvard Architect Questioned in Case of Missing Cambridge Girl, the *Globe* trumpeted on its front page the next morning, below the fold, but still hard to miss. A new picture of the photogenic Lara accompanied the article. This one showed her astride a bicycle, looking nervously at the camera with wide, innocent eyes. Next to her photo was a grainy image of a harried Xander leaving a building, the collar of his raincoat turned up, partially obscuring his face. Under the byline of Budge Buchanan, the *Globe* reported that "a world-famous architect from the Netherlands who is teaching this semester at the Harvard Graduate School of Design was brought in to Cambridge Police Headquarters Friday night to help the police with their investigation." Any connection the professor might have had with the girl wasn't mentioned. Yet.

Of all the scurrilous yellow journalism! Iris rolled up the paper and threw it across the kitchen into her small mud room. Sheba trotted off to fetch it and dropped it back at Iris' feet.

"No treat for you!"

It was now Saturday morning. Forty-eight hours had passed and Lara was still missing. Things were not looking good.

Iris flipped through her copy of the GSD staff directory and dialed Xander's number. It went straight to voice mail.

Ignoring Sheba's newly alert expression, Iris grabbed her jacket and headed out alone across Mass Ave toward Howland Street. Fifteen minutes later, as she approached Xander's house, she saw TV and newspaper trucks clogging the area. *Damn, the vultures have descended.* She hung back, considered her options, then veered off into a neighbor's driveway. With an assurance that implied she lived there, she headed toward a dilapidated, barely-standing detached garage that bordered Xander's fenced-in back yard. After skirting around the back of the garage, she considered her options. She tried calling him again and again was sent to voice mail. The small building hid her from the reporters as she approached the fence around Xander's backyard. She peered over and thought she saw him moving around in his kitchen. She waved her arms, but had little hope that he could see her.

She had to let him know that she had an alibi for him. He

shouldn't have to be treated like a suspect. If she could get through this fence, it would shield her from the reporters while she made her way to the rear entrance. Then she could knock on a window or door to get his attention.

After searching her pockets for a tool, she came up with a poop bag, some dog treats, a used tissue and a pencil. Nothing close to useful. So much for that. She squatted in the dirt, testing the wooden pickets. One plank was loose, so she worked it free, then used it to pry off three more, reminding herself to return with her tool kit later to repair the damage. She ducked through the small opening and scratched herself on a nail in the process. Creeping along the inside of the fence toward the kitchen door, she stayed low. She peeked through the upper glass pane of the door and spotted Xander, drinking coffee and running his hand through his hair. She rapped softly on the glass. He jumped up with a start, moved quickly to the door, and unlocked it for her.

"Iris, what are you doing here?" he whispered as he pulled her inside.

"I need to talk to you."

"I'm afraid this is not a good time."

"I know. I saw the reporters, I've read the paper, and I can help you. But first, I need to ask you something." Unasked, Iris took a seat. Xander joined her at the table, his place marked by a half-empty coffee cup and an ashtray brimming with butts.

"Really, Iris, it's kind of you but there's nothing you can do. I'm waiting for a call from the Dutch Consulate."

"Why did that girl come to your office last week?"

"How do you know about that? Were you the one who told the police that story?"

"No, but I saw her in the hall at GSD. Why did she come to see you?"

Xander looked directly into her eyes. "I have no idea. I'd never seen her before in my life."

Iris stared at him. "You don't know her?"

"I do not. I told that to the police."

"Did they ask you anything else?"

"I asked for a solicitor. That ended the discussion."

"Did you know of a solicitor, I mean a lawyer, to call?"

"Nils found me one who showed up within the hour. But as we left the police station, the reporters outside took pictures. They figured out who I am and somehow connected me to the case of the missing girl."

Iris exhaled loudly. "What a mess."

"Yes. Anyway, what is it you came to tell me?"

"I may be able to provide an alibi for you on Wednesday night if it turns out that you need one."

"But I didn't see you on Wednesday night. Unfortunately I was alone."

Iris tried to hide her chagrin behind a facade of innocence. "I was out taking my dog for her nightly walk on Wednesday. I went by the Bioscience building on Hammond Street to see how its construction was progressing, and I passed your house on my way back. The light was on. I was going to ring your bell to say hello but happened to glance in and see that you were listening to music so I decided not to disturb you."

Xander wore a strange, unreadable expression on his face.

What must he think of her? Iris willed herself not to blush. "Would you like me to explain this to the police?"

He looked perplexed, then said, "That's quite generous of you, Iris. Let me ask my solicitor. I find it hard to believe that I need to defend myself from this preposterous innuendo."

Xander's mobile phone buzzed and he walked off to the hallway to answer it.

Iris decided to give him his privacy. She had delivered her offer, at much cost to her pride. Now Xander probably thought she was some kind of groupie, stalking him, or worse.

Susan Cory

She'd now need to backtrack out of the house and off the property. She slipped out the kitchen door and hugged the house's back wall until she reached the fence. She ducked down and crawled along the perimeter until she arrived at the spot shielded by the neighbor's garage. She found the opening where she'd pried off the planks and squeezed through. She was just rising to her feet when a bright light blinded her. When her vision cleared, she could make out two dark forms standing in front of her and recognized the unmistakeable shrill voice of Budge Buchanon.

"Iris Reid? Is that you? What are YOU doing sneaking out of Xander DeWitt's back yard?"

CHAPTER FIFTEEN

Iris was squeezed into the front seat of Budge's compressed Fiat 500. She twisted sideways to face him. He had slipped her past the other reporters before they could register that she was one of the prey, not a fellow predator. *What did he intend to do with that photo?*

The *Globe* cameraman sat in the tiny back seat, his knees up to his chin, chain smoking out the partially opened window. Iris fanned away the secondary smoke.

Budge had moved the car around the corner to Wendell Street so they could talk in private, but now sat focused on his blackberry, thumbing in stacatto questions and reading the responses. After a few minutes he looked up. "So, you've been teaching this semester at GSD, alongside our mystery professor. You've come a long way, Iris, since our days at the Big D."

"You too, Budge." Iris eyed him cooly. "Down into the

depths of tabloid journalism."

"I'm Bobby now. Have you been following my story—on the front page? Looks like your friend has become a 'person of interest' to the cops. Why would a professor visiting from Europe have any connection to a twelve-year-old schoolgirl from some Bay State city? I know they have more liberal views on sexual mores in some of those countries. So, since you're obviously a close bud..."

"Professor DeWitt is a colleague. We had professional things to discuss this morning." Iris sat up tall, which wasn't easy to do in the dinky confines of a Fiat. It felt like the thing might tip over sideways. "I was trying to avoid the paparazzi phalanx you harpies created around the poor guy's house. I'm sure Professor DeWitt has had nothing to do with the missing girl. I don't know where you get your information, but I'd guess you'll be hearing from his lawyer about your article's, um, insinuations. Gee, you'd think you wrote for the *Herald* with that kind of mudslinging."

"We journalists just state the facts. For example, the fact that you were caught crawling through this guy's fence this morning—caught on film I might add—could well interest our readers."

Iris blanched. She could picture Luc's reaction. And what would her students think?

"Budge, if that photo ever shows up in print, my brother, the lawyer, will sue you personally, along with the paper, for libel. And I will hunt you down and string you up by your wretched little balls."

He cocked an eyebrow. "Whoa, Nellie—there's nothing libelous about printing a photo and telling people where it was taken. Our esteemed readers are free to draw their own conclusions."

Iris took a deep breath and counted to ten. Maybe she'd better try a more conciliatory approach. "Okay Budge. What do you want?"

"How about an exclusive interview with the professor? You get me that and we'll forget about your morning escapade."

Fuming, Iris grabbed her purse and slammed the car door behind her.

CHAPTER SIXTEEN

Iris marched back to her house, grabbed her gym bag and headed to her karate dojo a few blocks away on Mass Ave. She needed to punch something. Hard.

After wrapping on her gi and belt in the locker room, she entered the studio, bowing quickly at the portrait of Master Kanbun Uechi before sliding to her knees in the second row of brown belts just as her instructor, Sensei Ono, entered the room and kneeled, facing them. Iris had resumed attending karate classes after a fight for her life at her GSD reunion the previous summer. She'd forgotten how much she enjoyed the sense of strength it gave her.

They went through a series of stretches, conditioning drills, and katas, using movements of various sacred animals, before pairing off to practice their kicks. A beefy M.I.T. grad student she recognized from the occasional after-class bar crawl looped a cushion through his arm and braced himself to block her kicks as Sensei Ono began to shout out random heights for the students to strike.

"High."

She pictured Budge's face and she gave it a powerful roundhouse kick.

"Low."

She drilled into Budge's ankle with the side of her foot.

"Mid."

She grunted and nailed Budge's groin with the side of her heel.

"What did the guy do to make you so mad today?" her partner joked.

Iris tried to rein in her feelings and focus on her form before Sensei Ono wandered by to murmer some gentle restraining cautions. He'd often reminded them that this branch of karate was about self-defense, not attack.

They spent the rest of the class on Iris' favorite activity— sparring. She was again partnered with Mr. M.I.T. and was thrilled to be evenly matched in blocking kicks and delivering punches, despite his greater height and weight. Her signature move was a leg sweep, where she would get her opponent off balance by hooking his ankle, then yank him forward with one hand into a punch in the nose or chin by her other hand's palm. It required a great deal of control to stop the punches short of contact. Even with the padded head protectors and padded gloves, you could still injure your sparring partner if you couldn't pull your punch back in time. After half an hour, Iris was breathing hard and her skin glistened. By the time she tossed her red pads and gloves into their separate bins, she knew where she needed to go.

CHAPTER SEVENTEEN

Luc started most mornings at an ungodly hour—not even morning by Iris' definition. Meats were delivered from private farms two afternoons a week, but he needed an early start at his purveyors every morning except Sunday to gather the pick of the crops and the freshest seafood. After unloading his morning haul into the cold room next to the Paradise Café's kitchen, he would plan that day's dinner menu while sipping the first of several espressos at the Café's mahogany counter. Iris had fallen in with him the previous Spring when her own breakfast ritual at the Café had happened to intersect with his.

Despite Luc's prodigious caffeine consumption, he usually finished his mornings back in bed. So, that Saturday around noon, after her karate class and a quick shower in the dojo dressing room, Iris headed for his condo.

It hadn't really been a lie—not telling Luc about her dinner and lunches with Xander. It had been an error of omission. Or was it called a lie of omission? It wasn't as if anything had happened romantically.

She used her key so as not to wake him and, as expected, found him asleep in the bedroom. He was tangled in his sheets, breathing softly, with cheeks slightly pink, and his blond hair splayed across the pillow. His mouth was slightly open and she could see the crooked eye tooth she found so sexy. His eyes opened and he smiled up at her. "Take off your clothes. Come join me."

An hour later, Iris rummaged through leftovers in Luc's refrigerator for whatever might be interesting to throw into a frittata.

"Is this salmon still good?" She sniffed under the plastic wrap.

Hearing no response, she looked over at the table by the window to see Luc intently reading the *Globe*.

He didn't look up as he asked "Have you read about this lost girl, Lara? It mentions a GSD professor who might be involved—Xander DeWitt. Didn't you tell me you knew him?"

Here was her opening to come clean. "He's the visiting architect from Amsterdam I told you about. I read that article this morning but I can't imagine he'd be involved."

"How well do you know the guy?"

"He's a colleague. We've talked a bit. Everyone was pretty curious about him because of his reputation. There's talk he may win the next Pritzker Prize." She wasn't explaining this well.

Luc looked up at her. "Sounds like you admire the guy."

"Well, he is an amazing architect. It would be like you working alongside Ferran Adrià or René Redzepi."

"He's that kind of superstar?"

"He's up there. The guy's a real inspiration. When he's not designing beautiful buildings, he's writing poetry, or listening to music. God knows, he probably composes it, too. He makes me feel like an undisciplined slacker."

"Maybe he has a dark side. The police must think he knows something about the disappearance of this girl or they wouldn't be hauling him in for questioning. What would her connection be to him, unless she's a relative or something?"

" The girl stopped by his office looking for him when he wasn't there. Xander said he's never met her. He has no idea why she wanted to see her." Iris hadn't noticed that she'd slipped into dangerous territory until she saw Luc's cloudy expression.

"You've discussed this with him? When? The article only

came out this morning."

Damn, she was not defusing the situation. "I saw him this morning," she admitted.

Luc looked confused. "But it's Saturday. Did you go in to GSD this morning?" Then his expression turned to shock. "Wait— did you spend the night with this guy?"

"No—of course not. I just talked with him this morning as a friend. We'd had one dinner together..." Iris trailed off as she saw the hurt look on Luc's face.

"You're getting the wrong idea," she said. "It was a meal with a colleague—nothing more. I was curious about his work. Then I saw him briefly this morning." Her words sounded desperate, even to herself.

Luc sat rigidly, staring at the newspaper. After a minute he got up. "I need some air."

He walked out.

CHAPTER EIGHTEEN

Iris went home and collapsed at her kitchen table, her head in her hands. She felt sick.

If Luc was upset over the dinner she'd had with Xander, how would he feel tomorrow, seeing a photo in the newspaper of her furtive exit from Xander's house? It would look like she really had spent the night with him. She groaned and Sheba, startled, looked up from her favorite sleeping spot inside the kitchen fireplace.

Iris speed-dialed Ellie for advice, then pressed "end" before the call went through. It was time for Iris to sort out her own problems.

"I'll give Luc some space," she said to Sheba, "then go by the restaurant later to grovel. I need to prepare him before that photo shows up tomorrow."

The dog blinked up at Iris with liquid eyes.

"You're right, girl. First I'll behave like a responsible

professor and check on my AWOL student."

*   *   *

Iris ended up getting Jasna's address from the on-line student records. She navigated her Jeep through the streets of Cambridge, too accustomed to the pot-holes and patched pavement to give in to her natural urge to check for a flat tire. A few blocks from Fresh Pond Parkway she pulled up to a brick apartment building with peeling paint trim.

She was about to press the "Unit 3: Jasna Sidran" button above the mailboxes, when a harried young mother holding a mewling toddler bustled out through the inner door. Iris stuck her foot in the door before it closed. She figured Unit 3 to be on the second floor of a building this small. She couldn't help noticing a structural problem as she climbed a staircase which pitched downward from the outer wall.

The strong smell of curry filled the hallway. As Iris approached the door of Unit 3, she could hear someone's conversation in rapid French passing through into the hall.

"Where did you leave it?" said a voice that sounded like Jasna's. Iris hadn't thought of her as French.

Iris rapped on the door. The voice went silent but no one

answered. She knocked louder. "Jasna, it's Iris. I wanted to make sure you're okay."

After a moment, the door opened a crack. A sliver of Jasna's face appeared. The sockets under her eyes looked hollowed-out. Her skin was sallow.

"We've missed you in class these last few days," Iris said. "I wanted to make sure you weren't sick."

Jasna started coughing and backed away an inch or two. "I have the flu but I am getting better," she said a bit stiffly.

"Do you need anything? Some soup or juice?" Iris could now see enough of her student to notice some lines of blood on Jasna's bare outer thigh, below the girl's huge, paint-splattered t-shirt.

"It looks like you're hurt. Do you need me to drive you to Harvard Health?"

"No. I'm fine."

"But... " Iris tried to nudge the door open further with her foot.

"I will be in class Monday. Thank you for coming. I need to sleep now." Jasna pushed the door closed.

Iris trudged back to her car. Was the blood on her thighs from Jasna cutting herself? How could she get her troubled student to accept help?

She couldn't seem to do anything right today. She couldn't get Jasna to trust her, she had managed to hurt her lover's feelings, and now, to top it off, an embarassing photo of her would be in tomorrow's paper. She should've stayed in bed.

CHAPTER NINETEEN

Luc wouldn't return her calls to his condo, the café, or his cell. When Iris had broken down and called Ellie, her friend had assured her that Luc would relent. But when Iris told her about the kicker, that morning's visit to Xander, captured on film and set to be plastered in the *Globe*, even Ellie couldn't offer much optimism.

But at six that evening Ellie called back. "Iris, turn on the news. Channel 4. There's going to be an announcement about Xander's connection to the missing girl. It was on the banner that scrolls along the bottom of the TV."

Iris ran to her living room and fumbled with the remote. An overly-loud Bernie and Phil furniture commercial, usually producing a reflex jab to the mute button, was just ending. Then Xander appeared on the screen in an elegantly tailored suit. He closed his front door, then tried to make his way past a dozen reporters shouting questions and thrusting microphones toward him. Iris thought she could spot Budge's emerging bald spot among the heads.

At the top of the porch stairs Xander stopped, in a seemingly impromptu move, and said "I would like to clear something up. There's been speculation about a connection between me and the missing girl, Lara Kurjak. I do not know Lara, but was told she might have tried to come to my office last week. I've been searching my memory to try to find a reason for her visit and the only possible link I can come up with might stem from my days of military service in the Dutch division of the UN Peacekeeping Troops. I was stationed in Bosnia in 1994 through 1995. I was romantically involved with a Bosnian woman during my time there and since the dates seem to align, I can only speculate that this girl might be a product of that romance. I returned to Bosnia after the war to re-unite with this woman but, by that time, she had left her village and I couldn't find her. I was never told that there might have been a child. I want to repeat that I don't know if this was what happened, but it's the only scenario I can think of that might explain her coming to see me."

At this point Xander's dazzling blue eyes had turned misty and he looked off into space. The reporters seemed spellbound. Xander had taken on the air of a romantic hero, perhaps the lead from "Miss Saigon."

Xander snapped out of his trance and continued. "I would like the focus to be on finding Lara. That's all that matters now." Then he bustled down the steps and disappeared into a waiting taxi. The frenzied pack of reporters shouted unanswered questions at the departing vehicle.

CHAPTER TWENTY

After Xander's media "confession," Lara mania went into high gear throughout the Commonwealth. The idea of the lost girl being on the verge of finding her photogenic birth father seemed irresistible.

Iris was relieved to find no humiliating photo of herself in the Sunday paper. Not even a little one buried in the Metro section. Instead, the insufferable Budge had featured on the front page a noble-looking photo of Xander next to one of the troll-like Ivano Kurjak. The headline read ***Who is Lara's Real Father?***

Budge had interviewed Mr. Kurjak directly after the Saturday "bombshell," and the man had been apoplectic in his denials about any part Xander might have played in Lara's parentage after an affair with his wife. "The disrespect this man shows me!" he was quoted as shouting. "How dare he?"

Ever the conscientious reporter, Budge had done follow-up interviews with "persons on the street" reacting to Xander's speculations.

"Lara looks a lot more like that cute architect than the other guy. The cops need to find her so they can, you know, be a family," said Tiffany from Quincy.

"I think it's tragic. Poor kid gets nabbed from her own apartment. I hate that," said Ritchie from South Boston. "Oh, yeah. The Harvard guy. He needs to man up—get out there and find his kid."

"I pray for Lara. I'm sure the police are doing their best to bring her home to whichever man turns out to be her father. Poor thing doesn't have a mother," said Mrs. Edward Stritch from Scituate.

That last was the most noncommittal of the reactions that Budge offered up.

Iris took a bowl of oatmeal out of the microwave and put it in the freezer to cool.

"Sheba, Xander bumped us off the front page. Bless the man!"

Sheba, from her resting place inside the kitchen fireplace, raised her head at mention of her name, then sensing a rhetorical comment with no pathway to treats, lowered it again.

The memory of the photo Budge was holding over her head

brought a pang of guilt as Iris remembered how hurt Luc had looked. Even though she'd confessed to Luc that she'd spoken with Xander the previous morning, he still didn't need to see a photo of her sneaking out from under the guy's fence looking guilty-as-sin of something. She checked her watch. Nine in the morning was too early to wake him after his typical frantic Saturday night of cooking at the café. This was the only morning he had to sleep in, a Sunday with no trip to the food market, no suppliers to call.

Then again, maybe this was the perfect time to catch him with his guard down. She changed into black jeans and a sweater, then snapped Sheba's leash onto her pink leather collar with biker's studs.

As soon as Iris opened the door to Luc's condo, Sheba raced toward the bedroom. Only then did Iris pause. Was it such a great idea to barge in on Luc the morning after they'd had a disagreement? What if he had company? It wasn't as if they had ever discussed any ground rules for this relationship. After a month or so of spending nights together, Luc had simply given her a key. She had done the same.

Iris crept toward the door without hearing any voice, much less two. She peered in to see Sheba sitting on Luc's empty bed. The dog looked at her and let out a mournful howl.

Iris remembered, several Saturdays before, when she had swung by the restaurant at closing time to find two foxy, thirtyish women avidly chatting up Luc.

She slid under Luc's duvet and curled her body around his cold pillow.

CHAPTER 21

Detective Russo's stomach roiled in protest at his third cup of scorched police station coffee. It was Sunday morning and he tossed the front section of the *Globe* into the trash can. He ran his hand from the base of his short, powerful neck up over his shaved head and back again, which did nothing to relax him. The brass wanted Paul Malone to handle this Lara Kurjak case instead of Missing Persons. Since Malone was his lieutenant as well as his partner, the case was his as well. Russo hated these missing kids cases. He stared at the framed photograph on his desk of his red-headed son, ten-year-old Charlie Junior, in a little league uniform. If he had his way, knowing what he did about the pervs out there, he'd never let Charlie leave the house.

The media pressure was already starting to ramp up after that jerk Harvard professor had fanned the flames on TV the night before. Maybe this would give him the opportunity to show Malone how much he'd learned at those expensive Criminal Justice workshops he'd been going to. He could do more of the heavy lifting on the case before Malone went into his predictable uber-stressed mode, with all the weight loss, haunted looks, and wickedly short tempers that that went with it.

Russo heard an attention-seeking cough and glanced up at the ponytailed rookie, Samantha Carter, standing at the entrance to his cluttered workspace.

"There's a call on the helpline you might want to hear."

"Someone saw her?" he asked as he followed Carter to her cubicle in the open office section of the homicide division. He couldn't help thinking for the hundredth time since they'd moved to East Cambridge from the grand but seedy old HQ in Central Square that the new headquarters looked like a friggin' insurance office.

"No, it's about the father. He sounds like a real piece of work," she said.

"Caller?"

"Wouldn't identify herself but said the father knows her husband."

"Do we have a track on where she called from?"

"No, she hung up too soon."

Russo plonked himself down into a visitor chair that creaked slightly. Carter punched buttons as she listened to the left earphone of her headset.

"Here it is." She put the sound on speaker.

"Lara's father, Ivano Kurjak, told my husband he'd sold Lara to a man in Bosnia. He said he was going to send her there to marry this man after her school was finished in June."

Samantha's voice came on. "Ma'am, can you tell me your name and how your husband knows Mr. Kurjak?"

The raspy voice continued. "She probably tried to run away. He might have found her and smuggled her out of the country. That's what you should check on."

"Tell me your name please."

The line went dead.

"Could you trace it?" Russo asked.

"No, she must have been timing it. Why do the cop shows give away all our secrets? She rang off just before the address registered."

"Damn." Russo stood. "Still, good work, Carter. See if you can clean up the recording. Maybe there's some background noise we can use."

On his way back to his desk, the detective stopped at Malone's glass-enclosed office to update his superior. As Malone looked up from his bulky desktop computer and spotted Russo lingering in the doorway, he said, "How's it going tracking down our professor's war-time paramour?"

Russo eased into the office and relaxed into the chair across from Malone. "It's been really hard to track down any records from that time. Bosnia was the Wild West when DeWitt was out there."

"Were you able to dig up anything about his activities there?" Malone asked.

"He was in this division, the Dutchbat, that was assigned to protect the Muslims in Srebrenica. Thing is, they obviously failed because the Serbs ended up massacring eight thousand Muslim men and boys and raping most of the Muslim women."

"The Dutch soldiers just stood by and let that happen?"

"According to what I've read, these guys had their hands tied," Russo explained. "The UN would only let them use force in self-defense and the NATO planes that were supposed to do the actual fighting never showed up."

"Sounds like a scene from Hell. And we're supposed to believe that in the middle of all this DeWitt was playing Romeo with some Muslim woman?"

Russo shrugged. "I wouldn't know, but I guess these things happen during wartime. I did manage to come up with the name of someone from his division. The guy lives in London now. I left him a voice message several hours ago but he hasn't called me back yet, no surprise given the time difference."

"Good—keep ahead of that. And see if you can find out where the assistant Nils something was on that Wednesday night. Maybe he's the one Lara was really coming to see at the GSD."

Russo was about to rise from his chair when he remembered what he'd come here to tell Malone. "Almost forgot—Carter got an anonymous tip saying the father had promised the girl for an arranged marriage in Bosnia this summer. Can you believe it? The kid is twelve—she should be playing with dolls or maybe watching *Gossip Girl*."

Malone shook his head in disgust. "Get Foster to check the airlines for female minors traveling to that area in the last few days. Probably need to check flights to Paris and Frankfurt, too... who knows where else."

"Will do. But doesn't this give more weight to our idea that she's a runaway?"

"We're already following up on how she might have left the area. But, seems like time to bring dear old dad in for questioning."

CHAPTER 22

Ellie tapped on Iris' kitchen window and waggled a turquoise yoga mat in front of her.

As Iris let her in Ellie took in the scene and asked, "What's wrong? Are things still messed up with Luc?"

"Is it that obvious?"

"You're reading the obituaries," she stabbed the newspaper spread out on the kitchen table with her index finger, "while listening to Bonnie Raitt in the middle of a Sunday afternoon. I rest my case. Now go get on your yoga clothes and we can talk on the way over."

Five minutes later they were walking along Walden St. toward the Soni Yoga Studio.

"Don't jump to conclusions," Ellie said. "I can't see Luc spending the night with someone else. Jeez Iris, he made you that eight course meal of your favorite foods a few weeks ago. He even boiled up sticky toffee pudding for dessert! He loves you. Of course he's intimidated by your going out to dinner with one of the most famous architects in the world. You just need to assure him that Xander is not real life. Luc's your real life. You can get him settled down."

"I told him I wasn't interested in *dating* Xander. I was just curious about the life of a hotshot celebrity architect like him."

"You know you can be pretty intimidating yourself."

"Oh, please. You know me better than that," Iris said.

"Sure, I do. I know how insecure you can be and where your baggage comes from. But poor Luc doesn't. You need to show him that side of you."

"The screwed-up side."

"Exactly."

They unrolled their mats and spent the next hour saluting the sun and posing like mountains.

Looking at the front row, Iris recognized the gray braid of Alise, a favorite neighbor who sometimes dog-sat for Sheba. When the class was over, Alise joined them on their walk home. As they passed the community garden at the Raymond St. playground, Alise said "I am so in love with your boyfriend, Iris."

"Should I be worried?" Iris asked.

Alise chuckled. "Luc did a presentation this morning at the

garden here, giving us some great new ways to use herbs in cooking. I can't wait to try his recipe for elderflower sauce to put on shrimp."

"He was here this morning?"

"Yes, didn't you know? The posters were on telephone poles all around the neighborhood. He was so patient. One woman even brought her little granddaughter. He let the girl smell the different herbs. What a sweet guy."

Ellie gave Iris a sharp elbow in the ribs.

CHAPTER 23

Iris entered her kitchen bubbling and humming with affection for Luc. He WAS a sweet guy, and she was lucky. She needed to reassure him about her commitment to him, so she speed-dialed his number, and felt a thrill when he answered.

"Hi, it's me," she said. "Can I come over to talk?"

There was a gaping pause, then "I'm heading over to my sister's for dinner soon."

She let out a breath.

"But I have half an hour before I need to leave," he continued, "if you wanted to come over now."

"I'll be right there. Five minutes."

Iris ran up to her bedroom to peel off her sweaty yogawear and take a quick shower. She tossed on a loose cashmere sweater and a pair of skinny jeans, then shook her long chestnut hair out of its ponytail. Luc had sounded distant, maybe irritated. She had to smooth things over. After slapping on a swipe of red berry lip stain, she flew downstairs. She put Sheba on her leash, then opened the door. Only to find Jasna standing on the front porch, looking ashen, her spindly arm in mid-reach toward the doorbell.

"I'm just running out now," Iris blurted out before registering how debilitated her student looked.

"I need your help," Jasna said, her dark eyes pleading.

Iris checked her watch, then figured she could take a few minutes to calm her student's stress about whatever imagined catastrophe before setting off again for Luc's place. She led Jasna quickly into the living room.

Jasna perched on the edge of one of Iris' favorite black leather club chairs. "Please, I have to tell someone. This is all my fault and now Lara might be dead."

"Lara? The missing girl?" Iris settled onto the sofa across from Jasna. "How are you involved with her?"

"This is such a mess." Clearly at the point of tears, Jasna told Iris how she had befriended Lara and tried to help the girl escape from her father's plan for some awful hell of an arranged marriage in Bosnia.

"What about the police? Or child services? Why didn't you report this to them? They could have stopped the father."

"Lara was terrified they would put her in foster care, into

some group home or have her adopted by someone even more abusive than her father," Jasna explained. "She wanted me to adopt her, but I live too close by. Her father would have found her and shipped her off to Bosnia."

Iris had to concede that they were right—Lara probably would have ended up in foster care if she had approached any authorities at all."Okay, what happened next?"

"I noticed bruises on Lara's arms when I'd see her in her father's shop where she worked after school. He was hitting her when he got drunk. I knew I had to help her get away soon."

"Where were you intending to hide her?"

"I have a brother, Edvin, in another country. He and his partner love kids. We all talked about Lara going to live with them. She and Edvin hit it off when they met, and Lara liked the idea of being far enough away from her father."

"And something went wrong with this plan?" Iris said.

Jasna ran a hand through her choppy black hair until it stood up in tufts. "On the night Lara disappeared, she came to my apartment and waited there while I went to Rory's to borrow his car. I was only gone for half an hour. When I returned she was gone. The window to the fire escape was open and my bedspread was missing. Lara's bag, with all her things in it, was still there."

"Maybe she changed her mind and decided to run away?"

"That's what I'd hoped at first. I thought maybe she'd gotten scared about such a big, sudden change and gone instead to a friend's house. I kept hoping she'd call me in the morning. No call ever came and I got scared. Why would she have left all her things behind? She even left her wallet with some money. And we had already talked about other places she could go—there weren't any. She had no other choices."

"Call the police," Iris instructed. "Now. They need to have it confirmed that someone took Lara. They probably think she ran away."

"I already made a call to the police, anonymously, telling them about the arranged marriage threat."

"Good. They need to know that. Maybe her father learned about your plan, then followed her to your apartment and grabbed her. She could be in Bosnia by now."

"Then why would he have reported her missing to the police?" Jasna asked.

Iris considered the question, then said "that's something for the police to figure out. But they need to have all of the facts before they can track Lara down. Right now they don't even know an accurate location or time for where or when she went missing.

That means they're wasting their time questioning people around Lara's apartment about earlier that evening."

Jasna suddenly couldn't seem to catch her breath and started to hyperventilate.

Iris was on her feet and crossed the room to ease the girl's head gently down as she bent forward. "Stay there. I'll get a paper bag." She rushed back from her kitchen recycling bin and handed the Star Market bag to Jasna, telling her to "breathe deeply into this." Where Iris had learned that trick, she had no idea.

After a few minutes Jasna's panic attack gradually subsided and she sat back up. Her face was a mask of despair. "I *can't* tell this to the police. I was helping a minor run away. I'm here on a student visa and Immigration will deport me. Professor Reid, I need you to tell them. That's why I came here. But I need you to tell them without their finding out about me. Please?"

Iris knew she was susceptible to this kind of appeal. She knew she was a sucker for helping an underdog, and that it always got her into trouble. Yet she found herself saying "Maybe there's some indirect way of getting this information to the police. Let me think about it. But the first order of business now is to get you something to eat. You look like you haven't eaten or slept in days."

Jasna gave her a pathetic, grateful look. "I've just been so worried about Lara," she said.

Iris checked her watch. "It's eight-thirty. I don't have much in my refrigerator so I'm going to take you out to dinner."

Her words seemed to calm the young woman down. Iris grabbed her purse and jacket, then stood still before Jasna.

"There's one thing we need to get straight if I'm going to help you, one condition."

"Anything."

"I saw the marks on your legs yesterday. You're not going to be able to help Lara if you can't stay healthy yourself. So here's the deal. We'll look for Lara and you'll get some serious professional help for the cutting. OK?"

Jasna looked away. "I will." She wrapped her raincoat tighter around her small frame. "It's just that I just blame myself. She never would've been taken if it weren't for my stupid plan," she whispered.

"This is not your fault." Iris rested a hand on Jasna's shoulder reassuringly. "Her father's plan to send her to Bosnia is what started this chain of events. But the person to blame is whoever took her."

As they approached the front door Iris saw Sheba curled up in front of it, leash still attached.

"Oh, hell," Iris said as she remembered her overdue rendezvous with Luc.

CHAPTER 24

"You think Slavs are barbarians! This is ethnic profile. Who told you I sending my angel to Bosnia to marry? Is it the Dutch swine? He is telling more lies?"

Malone flicked a beleaguered look at his partner and pulled back from the table. They had been stuck in this cramped interview room for the last half hour with a truculent man who smelled like grease and onions. Worse, whenever the guy got excited, which was frequently, he would launch spit across the table along with his agitated words.

Malone rose to his feet and said, "Wanna Coke?"

"Yes, I want Coke," Mr. Kurjak said, folding his arms across his chest.

"Actually, I was asking the detective, but I'll get you one too." Malone slammed the door shut behind him.

"Look, Mr. Kurjak," Russo said, "we have a witness who told us about the arranged marriage in Bosnia. If you want to help us find your daughter, you need to tell us everything that was going on with her. Don't get me wrong, you have my sympathy. I'm sure it's difficult raising a young girl by yourself."

Kurjak exhaled a "Pfff."

"It must be stressful to try to run a business while taking care of a preteen girl. I can understand that." Russo tried to look solicitious. "You go to these card games with your friends. Have a few drinks".

"Hey, I don't drink alcohol and I don't gamble. We play cards, but not for money. I'm good Muslim."

"I understand. You don't drink, but you're playing cards, talking with your buddies. Maybe someone mentions that they have a friend back in the old country who needs a wife. Lara is a good Muslim daughter. She'd probably make a good wife. She's a beautiful girl, no?"

Ivano Kurjak glared at him from under his bushy eyebrows.

"So how did Lara take the news? Some girls might find it exciting, even romantic to get married that young."

Ivano's glare turned ominous. At least he hadn't lawyered up yet.

"How old was your wife when you married?"

Malone returned with three sweating soda cans that he

passed around.

"We can find that out in the records," Russo continued. "Does Lara have a passport?"

Kurjak offered nothing.

"We can check on that too."

After another fruitless twenty minutes, Malone indicated the door and said " Mr. Kurjak, you're free to go. Thank you so much for your co-operation. I hope we can count on you to help us if anything new develops."

As Lara's father was escorted onto the elevator, Officer Foster slipped in behind him, absently punching something into his phone.

Back in Malone's tidy office, Russo sat in the lone visitor's chair. "I pity poor Lara for having him for a father. Foster's the tail?"

"Yeah, let's see where Kurjak goes now that we've riled him up."

"So, no Amber Alert, right?" Russo asked.

"It doesn't meet the criteria. We can't even prove that an abduction's taken place. We sure as hell don't have a description of the captor or vehicle. She might be a runaway. We just haven't found her trail yet. It's times like these I almost wish the Feebs would muscle their way into the case."

The two detectives fell into a generally aggravated silence, as Malone randomly pushed some papers around his desktop. The phone buzzed. Malone listened for a few seconds, then gave Russo a get-up flick of his hand. "You've got the callback from London on your line—the guy from DeWitt's UN group."

A short while later Russo slid back into the extra chair across Malone's obsessively neat desk as the lieutenant gave him his full attention.

Russo's eyes were wide and he shook his head slowly. "I've just heard a complete re-enactment of how the Serbs held the Dutch peacekeepers hostage, demanding and getting all of the U.N. battalion's weapons."

"What?" Malone said. "The Serbs took the U.N. troops' guns? How did they get away with that?"

"Sounds like the Serbs did whatever they wanted." Russo shifted in his seat. "It gets worse. While the Dutch guys were unarmed, the Serbs marched into the protected safe area of Srebrenica and pretty much slaughtered all the male Muslims. You don't even want to know what they did to the females."

"Oh, God. This was on the news. Ethnic cleansing—right?"

"Yeah, the Serbs were on a mission. Meanwhile, the Dutch

soldiers had no weapons and couldn't do anything, and when they returned to Holland and they got treated like shit for letting it happen."

"And DeWitt was mixed up in this?"

"He was in the middle of it. Somehow, it doesn't sound like a setting for romance."

"Did this Brit from his battalion say anything about DeWitt's activities over there? Did he know of any Bosnian girlfriends or anything?"

"Said he'd never seen DeWitt with any woman—thought he was gay. He did say that the guy spent a lot of time off in the woods. He almost missed roll call once and that got him a detention, on-base for a day, a big deal, that. He remembered that because he didn't like the guy. He thought DeWitt gave off 'superior airs.' That's how he put it."

"Were there any other soldiers DeWitt was close with?"

"Apparently he saved a guy's life. A fellow Dutch soldier named 'Crazy-dog' Jansen. No one ever used his real name. A Serb sniper started shooting from a church tower in a village they were patrolling. Crazy-dog got shot in the leg. He was out in the open, an easy target, when DeWitt pulled him behind a truck, then dragged him to safety."

"So our professor is a war hero?"

"He did get a medal for it. The guy on the phone said that that just made him more insufferable. But the Jansen kid followed him around like a puppy for the rest of their time there."

"Did your caller have any idea where this Jansen guy is now?"

"As a matter of fact, he spotted him in some photograph in an article about DeWitt. Jansen works in DeWitt's office back in Amsterdam."

"See if you can track him down. Find out whatever you can about the professor's love life in Bosnia. Something doesn't smell right."

"Like what?"

"Like the girl going to the professor's office because she's learned he's her long-lost father."

CHAPTER 25

Around nine-thirty, after another excellent dinner in his own company at the Harvest, Xander walked home, deep in thought. Wednesday night had been a huge mistake. He shouldn't have had that bottle of 15-year-old Macallan in the house. Someone was trying to set him up and he still couldn't figure out who it was. He'd broken his own rule of one drink a night. But not by a lot. Hadn't he only had two? But then why had he passed out like that? Nils would kill him. It was a badly-kept secret that the Pritzker jury was considering him for next year's prize, and his assistant had made him promise to stay on his best behavior. Of course Xander wanted the award. He deserved it. It was part of his not-so-modest life plan perfectly timed for this exact stage in his career.

Xander turned onto his street and saw, lit up before him, the little house where he now lived. With it's simple gable roof, chimney and front porch, it looked like a child's drawing. He looked forward to curling up with a book in his living room's cocoon-like Swan chair. As he retrieved the keys from his pocket, he heard a loud creak on the porch deck behind him.

A large shadowy figure wrapped an arm around Xander's neck. Xander could feel his attacker's hot breath as the man whispered in his ear, "Tell me where you hide my girl."

Xander tried to wrestle out of the man's grip but he was trapped in a head-lock. "I don't have her," Xander spat out through clenched teeth.

"I'll make you tell the truth," Ivano Kurjak growled. "Cops can't do it, but I can."

Kurjak raised his right hand and struck Xander so hard he felt something in his neck crack. "That's for saying you screwed my wife."

Xander tried to scream for help, but couldn't draw any air into his lungs.

Kurjak grunted and delivered a ferocious punch to the man's ribs. The architect crashed into the side of the house.

"That's for what you've done to my girl."

As Xander crumpled to the ground, he tasted blood but managed to choke out, "I cannot tell you about something I did not do."

"So, you want the hard way."

Kurjak drilled his foot into his captive's back. Xander curled up into a ball. Ribbons of pain seared through him. He didn't want to think about what was coming next. He tried to focus instead on a way to escape, but fear paralyzed his brain.

And then, blessedly, a blue strobe light lit up the front yard.

"Kurjak, raise your arms above your head!" a booming voice commanded. "Drop to your knees."

Xander felt Kurjak's heavy steps running away across the porch decking and glimpsed a shadow chasing after him. He heard pounding in his ears, and then nothing.

*   *   *

Xander woke up in a hospital bed, feeling bruised all over. When he tried to sit up, sharp, burning stabs coursed through his back. He gasped and eased back against the pillows.

"Don't try to move." A tall woman with short, no-nonsense hair moved into his field of vision. She wore a concerned expression and seemed to be studying his pupils. "I'm Dr. Walker. You were brought here to Mt. Auburn Hospital after being assaulted. Do you remember what happened?"

Xander let out a moan at the memory of being beated up on

127

his porch. He could feel the compression of bandages encircling his abdomen. "What are my injuries?" he was able to croak.

"You've suffered a dislocated shoulder and a broken rib. We were concerned that you might have a ruptured kidney but the CT scan showed only a severe bruise. You will probably have some blood in your urine for a week or so. I've set your shoulder and your rib will heal gradually. You're on pain medication, which is why you feel woozy. If you need more, press this with your finger." She lifted the control button to show him. "It's regulated so you can't overdose."

"How did they find me? Who brought me here?" Xander asked, confused.

The doctor turned toward the doorway, where Xander now noticed the younger bald police detective. "You can ask this gentlemen those questions. I'll be back in an hour to check on you."

The detective put away the phone he'd been texting on, walked to the bedside, and squatted down beside the side rail.

"Did you get the bastard?" Xander asked.

"Yeah, we arrested Kurjak for assault and battery. Detective Foster saw everything."

"Yeah, he sat there and watched me getting beaten to a pulp."

"He needed to wait for back-up."

Xander considered this response. Had Foster taken his time, in case Kurjak could get Xander to talk, to tell where Lara was? That would have wrapped up their case pretty neatly.

"I hope you realize now that I'm innocent of any involvement with Lara," Xander said. "If I were guilty, surely I would have told that brute something in order to save my life."

"Unless you did something to his daughter that would've made him even more intent on working you over. All we've ruled out tonight is that it wasn't Kurjak who took Lara, unless he's a better actor than we think."

CHAPTER 26

Iris texted Luc from her tiny table in the bar area of Chez Jacques, a favorite Cuban bistro in her neighborhood. "So sorry. Emergency came up. I need to talk w/ u. XXOO, I." She deleted the XXOO, then put it back in and hit "send."

Iris nibbled on a plantain chip and thought again about ordering a Periodista. No, she would be driving and even one of those delicious rum drinks left her wobbly. She would need her wits about her tonight. The pressed duck sandwich had been dinner enough.

She looked over at Jasna, busy polishing off the last morsels of a Cuban sandwich and said, "Let's go over the timeframe from that night again." Iris thought back to the first news program she had seen about Lara's disappearance. "The police think she was taken from her apartment on May St. between seven and nine. When did you go to pick up Rory's car?"

"I left around nine forty-five and was gone for maybe half an hour, at most," Jasna said.

"This is critical information. Someone may have seen something later that night." Iris thought for a few moments, then asked "Do you know your neighbors? Are there any who walk dogs at night or who would have a reason to be out on the street at around ten o'clock?"

"There's a yappy dog above me that barks all day until the owner returns from work. He walks him at night, I think. At least then it's quiet for a little while."

"Good. We'll go talk to the neighbors. It's now nine-thirty—about the same time of night that Lara was taken. We can see who's outside tonight. If we can't tell the police the correct time she went missing, maybe we can ask around ourselves. It might make a difference."

After they both finished eating and Iris settled the bill, they drove over to Jasna's apartment in silence. Each was absorbed in her own thoughts. Iris' mind careened between frustration at missing the chance to clear the air with Luc to sadness over Jasna's story about Lara. Jasna's plan to help the girl escape her father had been so well intentioned. Iris needed to find a way to ease her student's guilt over the way it had all gone wrong. Finding the poor missing girl seemed like the only way to accomplish that.

The younger woman led Iris up the lop-sided staircase to the third floor. As Jasna knocked on her neighbor's door they heard a dog yapping wildly inside.

The security peephole in the door flicked, followed by a scowling face of indeterminate gender as the door opened a crack, stopped by the security chain. "I can't do nuthin' 'bout the barking. Sparky's just tellin' me it's time for his walk."

"I'm not here about the noise, Mr. Demopoulos. I was wondering if I might ask you something about last week." Jasna gestured toward Iris. "This is Professor Reid from my school. She's helping me search for a friend who has gone missing."

The gnome-like man eyed Iris suspiciously, then unhooked the door and opened it a few inches more. "I guess you can come in."

The apartment was strewn with newspapers. There seemed to be piles of them on every horizontal surface in the cramped living room. Sparky, a small, high-strung terrier, was hopping around his owner, all the while yapping and baring his teeth in menace.

"Your dog doesn't bite, does he?" Iris asked.

"Only if you try any funny business." The man bent down to pet Sparky. The dog seemed to begin foaming at the mouth.

Iris and Jasna hovered on the edges of arm chairs as Mr.

Demopoulos sat on top of a newspaper-covered sofa holding the wriggling dog in his arms. "I'm catching up on my reading," the man said as he waved an arm to encompass the room.

"Good idea," Jasna said. "Do you walk Sparky every night around this time?"

"Of course I do. A dog's gotta relieve himself at the end of a day. You'd know that if you were a dog lover."

Iris jumped in. "My dog, Sheba, goes out in my back yard around now too. We were wondering if you remember seeing anything unusual last Wednesday night when you took Sparky out. Did you notice any strangers around?"

"Wadda you mean, strangers? Some of these punk kids around here look pretty strange."

"No, I meant someone you didn't recognize from the neighborhood," Iris said.

Mr. Demopoulos patted Sparky while he thought. "Wednesday. Wednesday. What's on TV on Wednesday?"

Iris and Jasna looked at each other blankly until Iris remembered her own guilty-pleasure viewing that night.

"Urban Survivor."

"Oh, yeah. I love that show. But those poor kids. The things they have to find."

"So after you watched the kids looking for the cheese and the pig..."

"Hey, you watched the show too!"

"...you took Sparky outside." Iris prodded. "Did you happen to notice anyone new hanging around that night?"

"A new person? We mainly get the same neighborhood folks around here and the streets are pretty empty at that hour." The man scrunched up his face in concentration. "No, I don't remember anyone new that night."

Iris felt like shaking this guy. If Jasna's story was true, someone carried off Lara from this building right when this guy was out walking his dog, right under his nose."

"When you walk Sparky you go out the front door, right?" Jasna asked. "Do you walk back and forth in front of the building?"

"I mainly walk to that bush on the right when you go out. He does his business there, then we go back up. We're out there five minutes, tops. I didn't see no stranger out there Wednesday night, sorry."

They thanked the old man, tip-toed around the newspaper piles, and left. A few minutes later the two women sat on Jasna's front stoop lamenting their bad luck. "He must have just missed the kidnapping. Or else he's oblivious," Iris said.

"He probably only focuses on his dog and his newspapers," Jasna said. "Maybe I should show you the window that was open—where Lara was taken out."

Jasna led Iris to the alley alongside her building, then back to a yard that was a makeshift parking lot. She pointed to a fire escape. "See that light on the second floor? That's my bedroom. Lara was taken out of there."

Iris started up the rusty metal stairs, testing each step in front of her before committing her weight. Light spilling out of Jasna's bedroom lit their path. As they approached the window, a tiny yellow fragment caught Iris' eye. She got out her phone and pressed the flashlight app to illuminate it. A small scrap of fabric was wedged between the grate and side of the metal bars. Jasna leaned in and pried it out before Iris could say "Don't touch it. It's evidence!"

"But we can't give it to the police. We can't tell them about this," Jasna said as she held the material up to the light. "This is from my bedspread."

"That confirms your theory that she was taken out this back way. Maybe he wrapped her in the bedspread so no one could see her."

They didn't find anything else on the fire escape so they examined the area around its base. The dirt was too dry to show any footprints from four days before, or anything else for that matter.

They were still hunched over, inspecting the ground, when a back door opened to emit the squalling of an infant. A harried-looking man lurched out with a baby slung over his shoulder. He headed robotically toward a beat-up hatchback.

Jasna rushed up to him. "Hey Mark—can I ask you—were you out here last Wednesday night?"

The clearly exhausted man looked at her bleakly. "I'm out here every night. This kid won't sleep. She has colic. I have to drive her around in the car seat until she nods off. Sometimes it takes forty minutes of driving back and forth on Route 2. Why?"

"Did you happen to see anyone out here last Wednesday night?"

"You mean that jerk in the blue van? He almost ran me over."

CHAPTER 27

"You'd better be calling about that interview with DeWitt," Budge croaked. "It's six friggin' thirty in the morning, Reid."

Iris' brain felt fricaseed. She had stayed up late brainstorming with Jasna about how to trace the blue van's license plate, all of which Mark had miraculously remembered.

She rubbed her eyes with her free hand. "I've decided to let you know where you can find the professor alone so you can grill him to your heart's content. If you want to know where, meet me at Peet's. Over by Grendel's Den. Seven o'clock."

"Am I supposed to bring thirty pieces of silver or has he agreed to this interview?"

"I'll fill you in at Peet's and let you know my price."

"Intriguing. Make it seven-thirty. But don't forget I've still got that photograph of you, all ready for the front page."

After a long hot shower, during which she nearly fell back

asleep, followed by a hard splash of cold water, Iris walked the twenty minutes into Harvard Square. Better that than spending time circling to find a parking spot. She wound her scarf around her neck against the brisk October chill as she hurried along Mass Ave. A hunched-over bicyclist sped through a red light narrowly avoiding a collision with an SUV driver who'd over-anticipated his green. A horn blared and middle fingers were raised. Iris passed the brick Georgian facades of Harvard Yard on her left and navigated through the craziness of the Square's kamikaze traffic.

The aroma of coffee was palpable as she entered the café and scanned the room for Budge. Having arrived first, she joined the line to place her order—a triple espresso for her, an American regular for him, guessing at his preference.

Iris sipped fast and waited for the caffeine to reach her brain. She stared out the window at a ruddy-faced man asleep on a bench in Winthrop Park, covered in a tangle of sweaters and dirty jackets. She contemplated the plan they had come up with to find Lara quickly, without exposing Jasna's involvement. Why wasn't there another way that didn't involve Budge? This felt like making a deal with the Devil. Still, she felt confident that Xander had nothing to hide so what harm would it do to give him a chance to set the press straight?

She was just reaching to help herself to Budge's coffee when the devil himself appeared at the table.

"How do I know that he'll answer my questions?" he asked, shrugging off his overlarge overcoat.

"Use your journalistic skills, Budge. Here, have some coffee." She shoved the second cup at him.

He went to get more sugar at the supply table. His hair was wet and slicked back. With his protuding eyes he looked like a toad.

"Great place to meet," he said on his return. "Parking's fun at this hour."

"You'll soon learn why I picked it. "

Budge's eyes lit up. "Go ahead. I'm listening."

"First, you need to agree to do me a favor."

"Destroy the photo of you?"

"Yes, but that's understood. I need you to run a license plate for me. Some jerk nicked my car in the Star Market parking lot. Porter Square of course. A witness left me a note with the license number. I figure I might as well get something out of this scoop I'm giving you."

"Which might not pay off. He could just stonewall me. But if I do squeeze some sound bites out of him, I'll check your plate number with my source in the RMV."

Budge made a let's-move-this-along gesture with his hand.

"DeWitt swims every morning at eight at the Malkin Pool at Harvard. It's three blocks from here." She jerked her thumb across the small park. "You can pick up a Speedo at the Coop on your way. You'll have him all to yourself."

Budge took out his phone and checked the time."I'd better get going. I've got to get set up."

Then he turned to her with a skeptical look. "I thought this guy was a friend of yours."

"He is and you might be able to help him clear his name."

Budge regarded her intently then said, "Okay. Give me that license plate number."

CHAPTER 28

Iris spotted Luc sitting behind the mahogany coffee counter of his café, hunched over his laptop. He'd cut his hair. He looked so vulnerable with his gorgeous shoulder-length hair chopped off into a conventional "any guy" hairstyle. It had been only two days since she'd seen him but it felt to Iris like a war had intervened.

"Hey," she said.

His head jerked up and his mouth tightened.

"Can we talk?" she asked.

"I thought we were going to do that last night."

"Sorry, a student showed up with a personal emergency just as I was leaving the house."

Luc rose slowly and led her to a table in the corner. The few patrons there, mid-afternoon on a Monday, were lost in either a book or a laptop while sipping their coffee.

Sitting across from Luc, Iris wanted to reach for his hand but didn't dare risk him pulling away. "It was the young woman I've been telling you about, the loner."

He regarded her, waiting.

"Oh, hell. I'm not supposed to tell anyone, but I need you to understand what it was that kept me from coming over last night, Luc. This student is tangled up in the missing Lara business. She was trying to help Lara escape from her abusive father. Iris went on to fill in the rest of the story.

Luc listened to her carefully, relaxing a bit as she spoke. He was quiet for a moment, then he asked, "Why is she involving you?"

"She's on a student visa and thinks she'll get deported if the authorities learn she was somehow involved in this kidnapping. She's also terrified about what the father and his friends will do to her if they learn she was helping Lara run away."

Luc spoke slowly, "She's keeping information from the police that could help them find Lara, and you could be charged as an accessory to kidnapping for not reporting it."

Iris sighed. "Yeah. Could be. But if you'd have heard her story you'd have tried to help her too. We spent half the night trying to figure out how we could find Lara ourselves. We ended up talking to her neighbors and then we found someone who saw a van racing away from the building that night. That neighbor even remembered the license plate number because the van almost ran him over. So, this morning I met with the *Globe* reporter covering the Lara story and gave him the license number so he could track down whoever owns the van."

Luc looked off toward the window facing Mass Ave. "I can see that you have bigger things on your mind now than our personal issues." He dropped his gaze. "Why are you even with me, Iris?"

Iris felt an overwhelming ache inside her. "Because I love you."

"But we're so different. We're from different worlds."

"What do you mean?"

"You're from a family of academics. You went to Ivy League schools. My father was a cop. I didn't go to Harvard, I went to cooking school."

"Those things don't matter. You view your work and your passion as professionally as I do."

He looked up to face her. "But am I just a fling?"

Iris could feel him drifting away. She had to reel him back. "Wanting to observe DeWitt's life more closely was about questioning decisions I've made with my career. I was never questioning being with you. Listen to me, Luc—"

Iris stopped speaking when she saw Allegra, Luc's grandmotherly assistant chef, bustling towards their table.

"Luca, c'é una chiamata dal' estero per te in cucina," she called out.

"Use English, Allegra. Who's on the phone?"

"Is your wife!" She looked nervously at Iris, then scurried back into the kitchen.

Iris waited for Luc to correct the woman's terminology. Instead, looking grim, he avoided her eyes as he followed Allegra through the swinging door.

Iris sat in stunned silence as she let the exchange sink in. Then she skidded her chair away and crashed into a table on her way out.

CHAPTER 29

*H*ow far could she trust Iris? Jasna rubbed her eyes against the morning sun. She knew she'd taken a risk telling Iris about her plan to help Lara run away.

Even though the night had been far too short, she'd slept better than she had since this whole thing had begun. Maybe it was the relief of getting the search for Lara under way. Now she sat on her bed, propped against the pillows, trying not to focus on the prickliness of her skin. Earlier, she had forced herself to cook up some scrambled eggs to help get her strength back. Above all she needed to keep her mind lucid.

Iris had called Jasna after the morning meeting with the reporter to say that she thought the guy had taken the bait without questioning what the license plate request was really about.

Now they would track down the blue van's owner.

Iris had urged Jasna to take care of herself, but the tickling, tingling sensation would not go away. *You know what you need,* she heard the voice saying.

Just like that she was back there— smelling the pine trees in the Bosnian woods. It was the day she and her brother had been searching for coats.

The memory compelled her to rise and walk over to her wooden drafting table. She picked up the tiny, razor-sharp X-acto knife she kept in a wooden box.

The bastard Serbs had piled the Muslim bodies in shallow graves. She and Edvin would wash the coats in the stream if they did not have too much blood on them, or bullet holes, then barter them for food.

Jasna peeled off her sweat pants and tee shirt carefully, folding them onto a chair, then lay back on the bed. Her thighs were covered with aging hieroglyphic networks of delicate scars.

She remembered being so hungry during the war. To this day she would vomit if she had to eat another mushroom. She had wandered away from Edvin thinking she saw a bush with edible berries. She'd heard a rustling in the bushes—maybe a squirrel? That's when the man had grabbed her.

Jasna drew the blade slowly across her white flesh and felt release mingled with pain. She pressed down a tissue to staunch the oozing blood, and lay back against the pillows.

She could deal with this awful compulsion to cut herself later. For now, it felt good to have told Iris Reid part of the story.

CHAPTER 30

Detective Malone stopped by Russo's workstation on Tuesday morning and perched on the corner of his desk. "Looks like the father's gonna be locked up for quite awhile. But on another front, we've caught a break. I just got a call from our Feeb friend, Carlyle."

Russo swiveled around in his seat to face his partner. "It's the assistant, isn't it?"

"No—his alibi checked out. He was at that bar in the South End. Carlyle, got a hit from a kiddie porn site he was monitoring. After following the satellite pings through half of Eastern Europe, it bounced back to DeWitt's address."

Russo whistled. "The prof's a pedophile?"

"Affirmative. Carlyle's giving us a heads-up because he knows from the press that we're interested in him, too. The porn was of pre-teen girls, sick stuff. They got a warrant to take his computer and passport, but I convinced Carlyle to have the FBI watch and wait instead. We can't spook DeWitt before he leads us to the girl."

"DeWitt didn't give up anything when the father was wailing on him," Russo pointed out. "Then again, maybe he had nothing to admit that wouldn't have made things worse."

"We'll nail him now. But we've got to find the girl—she's priority #1. Judge Taylor is issuing a 'sneak and peek' warrant using the kiddie porn as probable cause. DeWitt was released from the hospital yesterday so he's probably teaching this afternoon. I need you to confirm that he's not at home."

"I can do that. What exactly will we be looking for?"

"Anything that can tie him to the girl. He claims he doesn't have a car. We need to find out if he has access to one. "

"If this guy's a predator and he sees us closing in, I doubt he'll keep the girl alive."

"That's why we're using a 'sneak and peek.' You and I are going to comb through the place, but leave it so he never knows we've been there. Nice and neat."

"I can't believe Interpol didn't turn up anything on him."

"This guy knows how to cover his tracks. To a point. After all, the Feebs traced him to the porn site."

CHAPTER 31

Iris ducked into Budge's tiny Fiat parked in her driveway. "How did your interview go with Professor DeWitt?"

"He never showed. Great tip, Reid."

"But he swims there every morning. Maybe he got lucky last night and decided to sleep in. Try him at the pool tomorrow. He told me he goes there every day." Iris took out a pad and pen from her pocket. "Can I get my information on credit? Were you able to find out who the guy was who hit my car?"

"That's the strange thing, Iris. I see two cars here in your driveway—a Jeep and a very cool Porsche. Neither of them shows any sign of damage."

"I already got the bodywork done."

Budge's look turned into *Oh, come on.*

"What do you care why I want it? Maybe the car belongs to a hot guy I saw driving around."

"As much as I'd like to help you with your love life, Iris, it's worth my job to track down license plates. But my spidey sense tells me this one's connected to an important story."

Iris swore inwardly. She needed that name. Lara's life might depend on it.

"If I tell you something off the record," Iris said, "will you keep my source's identity out of this?"

"Journalism 101, Reid—always protect your source."

"We're not talking Dustin Hoffman and Robert Redford here. We're talking you, Budge. Would you go to jail to protect this source?"

"Jeez, Iris. What have you gotten yourself into?"

"We're talking a missing twelve year old girl and how the police have the wrong idea about when and where she was taken."

Budge let out a low whistle. "The Lara story. My story." He thought for a minute. "OK, I'll protect the source if I can, but I won't jeopardize the girl's life."

"Fair enough." Iris exhaled. "Lara went to a friend's house after her father went out to play cards that night. She was taken from the friend's house closer to ten o'clock, not nine. The friend heard about a blue van with this license plate speeding off from her apartment building at ten that night."

"Why hasn't the friend told this to the cops? He's obstructing the investigation."

"I can't explain, it would jeopardize the friend. Can't you say that you got an anonymous tip with this information?"

Budge narrowed his eyes. "The cops would be all over how the tip came in. A lot has changed since Hoffman and Redford's day. Besides, my editor would never run an unsubstantiated story."

"So what are we going to do?"

Budge looked at her sideways. "Suddenly it's 'we'?"

"Come on, Budge. I told you my blockbuster. Now tell me who owns the van."

"Have you heard of a Harvard History professor named Stuart Kunstler?"

"I don't know many other profs unless they teach at GSD, and he's not one of the big names."

"He's on sabbatical in Turkey writing his next book," Budge said.

"Then he obviously wasn't driving a van here in Cambridge last week unless he made a quick trip home."

"The more important detail is where he lives." Budge paused for dramatic effect.

"Out with it."

"He lives at 8 Howland St. In other words, he's Xander DeWitt's neighbor."

CHAPTER 32

"**M**alone, come check this out," Russo called as he spotted a set of keys, half hidden in a jumble of tools in the back of a drawer in Xander DeWitt's kitchen.

Malone thumped down the stairs from the second floor and inspected Russo's find. "Bingo," he said. He uncurled a paper clip from his pocket and used it to lift a keyring gingerly. "This one's for a GMC vehicle. That second one looks like it goes to a padlock."

"You think it's for a locker?"

"Or maybe a garage. One of those old-fashioned ones with swinging doors."

Malone's attention moved to the keyring itself— some kind of dog with a big jaw. "D'you know if this dog is a sports mascot?"

Russo peered at it closely. "It's no team I've ever followed. Maybe a college mascot. Look, it's got a number scratched into the back, an eight. Think it could be an address?"

"Eight Howland Street is right next door. Let's see if there's a padlock on their garage when we leave. Photograph these keys before you put them back, and log in where they were. We can always come back and get them if it looks like they'll fit the neighbor's garage."

"Maybe we'll get lucky and find a vehicle with the professor's prints on it. Then so much for his story about not having access to a car."

An hour later they had searched the compact house from attic to basement and were finishing up in the study. Malone was flipping through a Dutch passport.

"Tell me why DeWitt flies to Bangkok once or twice a year."

"He likes Thai food?"

"Bangkok is a mecca for the underage sex trade."

A laptop sat on the desk. Malone eased himself into the leather desk chair, looked carefully around the edge of the computer, and flipped it open. "Password, password. What could it be? Too bad we couldn't spring loose a techie to come with us."

Russo was rifling through the CDs on a bookshelf. "Lots of classical stuff." He moved on to some audiobook CDs. "Hey, look at this one—Lolita. I think I saw the movie. Wasn't it about a pedophile?"

"Right," Malone said. "It's by Nabokov. Actually, according to an old girlfriend of mine, it's great literature."

Malone typed "Lolita" in the password box. An error message appeared.

He typed in "Nabokov." Again, no joy. That would have been too easy. He snapped the laptop's lid closed.

They completed their search in the small vestibule by the kitchen door. Malone noticed a pair of boots sitting on a mat. "These are the only things in the whole house that aren't immaculate. I can't believe that a guy lives here! Scrape off some of the crud from the soles and bag it for the lab, will you, Russo?"

They went out quietly through the back door so as not to attract attention from the neighbors, but as they followed the path along the side of the house they heard excited voices coming from the backyard on the other side of a tall fence.

"I can't believe you talked me into this, Reid!"

"We know he's on sabbatical in Turkey. It's not like anyone's going to notice us looking in the garage's windows. I just want to see if the blue van is in there."

Malone and Russo crept closer to the voices. Malone peeked above the fence to see a man and a woman peering in the side window of a detached garage belonging to DeWitt's neighbor.

Malone broke into a run around the fence, Russo at his heels. They both had their hands resting on their Glocks.

"Freeze!" Malone commanded. Budge and Iris stared at him, wide-eyed, and shot their hands in the air.

CHAPTER 33

"Don't say anything, Budge. My brother's a lawyer. He'll get us out of this," Iris hissed under her breath.

"No talking, you two! Ms. Reid, stand over there," Malone pointed to a spot on the gravel driveway. "You can put your hands down. Russo, get those keys. Use the gloves."

Malone approached the dirty garage window and cupped his hands to see inside.

"Ms. Reid," he said turning to face her, "you continue to turn up in interesting places."

"I'm teaching nearby." She waved in the direction of GSD. "Actually, I've got to get going right now. I have to get ready for my afternoon class."

"Not so fast. We'll be needing some answers from you." Malone pivoted to Budge. "And you, sir. Can I see some form of I.D. please?"

Budge reached into his pocket and surgically opened his

159

wallet to display his press pass.

Malone looked at him sharply. "The reporter on the Lara Kurjak story."

"Yes, sir," Budge answered.

Russo returned with the small ring of keys and fitted one into the padlock that secured the garage doors. The lock clicked, and hung, open-jawed from its hasp.

He swung the large doors open and light flooded the space. Through the cloud of fine dust, Iris saw a van with a dented back fender. As she moved closer, she could see that the van was blue. She and Budge drew sharp breaths at the same time. The license plate matched the number Jasna's neighbor had recited.

"What is it?" Malone looked from them to the license plate and back.

Iris' mind raced. The police found these keys in Xander's house. This van took Lara away.

Iris had a sickening feeling in the pit of her stomach. Had she befriended a kidnapping pedophile?

Russo circled the vehicle looking inside its windows, then shook his head in the negative. Malone murmered into his phone: "We need a Crime Scene team down here at 8 Howland St. Also, clear two interview rooms. I'm bringing some people back with us."

*   *   *

Two hours later, Iris stalked out of Cambridge Police Headquarters.

Her brother, Sterling, raised both palms in surrender. "You do realize that you've all three obstructed justice in a kidnapping case, don't you? Your student knew what really happened to Lara for five whole days and didn't tell the police. The cops thought the girl might have run away. They could have been following leads. They canvassed the wrong neighborhood. God only knows what this kid may have gone through in those five days."

"Stop it! I know I made a misjudgment. Jasna came to me, terrified. I tried to help her without getting her into trouble. Now things are even more messed up." She slumped onto the curb and put her head in her hands.

"It was only four months ago that I had to get you out of this same Police Station on a murder charge. Do you think I wait around my office all day for my sister's phone calls from jail? You're always doing this—trying to save some lost cause and making things worse. I remember that time you were in fourth

161

grade..."

Iris emitted muffled sobs.

"Stop crying," he said as he passed her one of the starched pocket squares he always sported in the breast pocket of his impeccable suits. He helped her to her feet.

"Now Jasna might be sent to jail," Iris said. "At the least she'll be a target for the father's Bosnian cronies, and get her student visa revoked. Why did you have to tell the police her name?"

"Your reporter friend didn't leave me much choice. He had the *Globe*'s attorney down here before I could even back my car out of my downtown parking lot. His attorney offered up everything but the girl's name in order to get his client off the hook. All I had left to work with was her identity."

"Sterling, please help her. Can't you get her immunity if she tells them the whole story?"

"At this point she'll get jail time if she doesn't tell them the whole story. And you'd be sitting in a holding cell now if I hadn't told them her name."

"Won't you represent her? Please, Sterling. I'll pay you."

"You can't afford me."

"Let me call her cell phone and reassure her that you'll meet her here. I'll warn her not to say anything. The police probably haven't reached her apartment yet."

Sterling stood stock still for a minute looking pained. "Why is Harvard hiring kidnappers as professors? We never had this problem at Yale."

CHAPTER 34

Iris trudged up Arlington St. from the Porter Square T, fighting the urge to stop at the Paradise Café to talk to Luc on the way. His betrayal coiled in the pit of her stomach. She rang Ellie's doorbell, praying her friend was home.

As soon as she saw Ellie's face in the door glass, a tear dribbled down Iris' cheek.

"He's married." Iris said when the door opened, then headed down the hall toward the kitchen at the back of Ellie's Victorian house.

"What? Who?" Ellie scurried after her.

"Luc. He's married," Iris said, dropping into a stool at the island and wiping away the tear.

Ellie drew back and stared at Iris. "No, he's not. Who told you that?"

"We were in the café talking. Allegra came out of the kitchen and told him he had a phone call. From his wife!"

"You know how bad Allegra's English is. She probably meant his mother."

"No. He didn't contradict her."

"What happened next?" Ellie eased into the stool next to her.

"He didn't look at me—just rushed off to answer the phone, so I got up and left." Iris rubbed the bruise on her thigh caused by her awkward exit.

Ellie opened her mouth, then closed it. Finally she said "Have you had lunch? I'll make us some sandwiches and we'll figure this out."

"I couldn't possibly eat. I'm too upset."

"There's got to be some other explanation. You and Luc have been practically living together. How could he be hiding a wife?"

"I must be so stupid." Iris dropped her head into her hands. "There's more." She filled Ellie in on Jasna's story.

"Jeez. Why didn't she go to the police? Why is she dragging you into it?"

Iris told Ellie about Jasna's fears and about how their attempts to track down the kidnapper's van ended in a trip to Police Headquarters and an emergency call to Sterling.

"How can you possibly pack that much drama into one day, Iris? Your life is like that TV show, '24.' Let me get my head around this. Xander might be involved with the kidnapping? Maybe we shouldn't jump to conclusions. Who knows how many garage keys the professor on sabbatical gave out to neighbors. If Xander were a pedophile wouldn't this have come out before? He's a public figure."

Iris wandered over to the freezer and returned with a pint of Toscanini's Burnt Caramel ice cream and two spoons.

"Wait a minute—you saw Xander on the night she was taken, didn't you?" Ellie asked, grabbing a spoon.

"I saw him at nine that night. But the police gave out a mistaken time because they didn't know the girl had been taken from Jasna's house an hour later."

"That was pretty critical information for Jasna to hold back. She might have kept the police from finding Lara while the trail was hot."

"I know, and now she's in a lot of trouble. Jasna and I were trying to track down Lara ourselves so she wouldn't be implicated. At least I convinced Sterling to represent her and to try to work something out with the police."

"This is a big deal, Iris." Ellie's eyes were serious. "Xander is a god in the architecture world. The trail you discovered has led the police to Xander and now Budge is going to splash the story all over Boston. Then the international papers will pick it up. If he really took Lara, then maybe the police can get him to say where she is now. But if he isn't involved, Xander's reputation will be destroyed."

Iris looked at her miserably. "I know. People's lives might be ruined and I feel responsible. Jasna came to me last night. Now, thanks to my brilliant 'help' she might get thrown in jail, and I've given a reporter ammunition that could ruin Xander's life. I still can't believe he's guilty. He didn't seem like a guy getting ready to go kidnap a twelve year old girl."

"The police can't arrest him just because he has a connection to the van. And Sterling's a shark, Iris. If anyone can help Jasna, he can."

Iris nodded. "That's my big brother—the shark you want swimming out in front of you in dangerous waters."

"As for Xander, I doubt that Budge will risk printing anything libelous."

"Just laying out the facts will sound incriminating enough."

Ellie smiled wanly. "There's one ray of sunshine. Luc won't be jealous of Xander after the *Globe* story comes out."

CHAPTER 35

"Uh, huh. Uh, huh." Russo held the phone loosely in his hand and stared at a tiny brown stain on the corner of an acoustical tile above his desk. It seemed to be spreading but he couldn't be sure. "Did you give copies of your garage key to anyone else, Professor Kunstler? ... Okay. By any chance, did you happen to keep track of how many miles were on the vehicle before you left in September? Really? And the inspection report is in the glove compartment? ... Got it— two trips to Star market after that. The Porter Square Star Market or the Beacon St. one? Okay. This is very helpful."

Malone poked his head into the cubicle, then leaned against a low partition to wait, arms folded.

"No, no. There's nothing wrong with the van," Russo continued. "There was a car stolen in your neighborhood. Kids going for a joy-ride. Would you do me a favor, professor? Would you please not mention our conversation to Professor DeWitt? No need to worry him. Thank you for your time. Bye now."

Russo digested the information. "We may be getting somewhere. I'll check the odometer, then see if I can get Crime Scene to send over the contents of the glove compartment, after they're done fingerprinting."

"Sounds like you're making some headway," Malone said. "Maybe I can light a fire under the goddamn Crime Lab to analyze the crud we got off DeWitt's boots and the van's tire treads. We've got to make up time since this idiot woman sat on the real kidnapping story for five days! What kind of a moron does that? Where is she, anyway?"

"Jackson and Lee went to her apartment to pick her up." Russo unwrapped a stick of gum and popped it into his mouth. "At least the Reid woman led us to the vehicle. Do you still want me to track down that 'Crazy-dog' guy who works in DeWitt's Amsterdam office?"

"Absolutely. We need to interview everyone who knows anything about the professor."

"Let me call their office manager again. She never returned my call. Meanwhile, are we going to let DeWitt stay free-range? No grabbing his phone or computer based on his lying about the van?"

"Foster's got eyes on him. We need him to lead us to the girl."

CHAPTER 36

Iris felt a bit more settled after leaving Ellie's. They had gotten through to her brother Sterling and, while he couldn't reassure them about Jasna's fate, it sounded like he was giving the case his full attention.

Iris walked up the hill to her own home to find Sheba waiting for her with an accusing look. The dog waddled over to her water bowl and stuck a paw in the bone-dry interior.

"Sorry, Shebz. I'm screwing up on all fronts today." Iris filled the bowl and gave the basset-hound a rolled-up chicken treat. Sheba took it indifferently from Iris' hand and walked around the corner to the office rug. For her own treat Iris tamped down a scoop of rich espresso into a sleek stainless steel pot, added water, and set it on the stove to heat. After waiting through a few moments of hissing and steam she poured the aromatic liquid into an all-black Wedgewood cup and headed into her office in the house's turreted corner room.

171

I need to do something productive today. She sat at her computer desk intending to check e-mails but her eyes drifted to her inspiration board on the wall behind the monitor. On it were tacked images that gave her pleasure— a museum in Verona by Carlo Scarpa, a light installation by James Turrell, a photograph of the Alhambra in Granada that she had taken at dusk . While nothing from these images moved directly into her designs, she believed that they influenced her in deeper ways, helping her to move conceptually beyond mere problem solving. Her first sketches of the Mt. Auburn Street townhouse project were pinned along one edge of the board. Her final design had neatly captured those early ideas, and melded the functional program and sculptural shapes to the unique qualities of the site.

Along one side wall hung a five foot tall mahogany sculpture that she had made in college. It resembled a set of abstract ubdulating wings. She had spent weeks sanding and oiling its surface until it seemed to glow from within. Years later, she still loved to run her hands over it.

Iris moved toward the large desk she had built, with a center section that flipped up into a drafting surface. She sat down to work on the electrical drawings for the townhouse and was soon absorbed in a world of technical problems to be solved.

It was hours later when she heard ringing from a long way off. She had to refocus her eyes to find her office phone.

She almost didn't recognize his voice at first, but then her heart started racing wildly.

Xander spoke with urgency: "Iris, I need to meet with you."

CHAPTER 37

"What should I do?" Iris whispered to Detective Malone. "I told him I was on the other line and needed to call him back."

"You don't need to whisper. He can't hear us," Malone said. "Are you willing to meet with him— in a public place, of course? We could wire you up and have our people nearby."

"That sounds dangerous. Wait a minute. Didn't I read it was illegal to tape someone without their consent in Massachusetts?"

"This is a police investigation. We're exempt from that statute."

The wheels turned in her brain and she was quiet for a moment, chewing her lip. "I'll do it on one condition—full immunity for Jasna, signed off by the District Attorney."

"Well...ok, if you can get us information that leads to Lara we'll see what we can do about Ms. Sidron's obstruction of justice charge."

Iris was quiet for a moment, then took a deep breath. "Not good enough. If I'm going to risk my life meeting with some kind of kidnapping pedophile, I'll need written assurance that Jasna won't be brought up on any charges. You can prep me with whatever questions you want me to ask him. Whether that leads to useful information or not isn't part of the deal. You know that this is your best chance at getting to him while his guard is down. Agreed?"

"Why does everyone watch cop shows nowadays? Good God. I'll call you back after I talk to the D.A. Meanwhile, think about a meeting place where you'll feel comfortable."

For a crazy second Iris thought of the Paradise café. She used to feel comfortable there.

A few minutes later Malone called her back. "I got a green light on the deal."

Iris clenched her fist and pumped her arm down in a silent "Yes!" She couldn't wait to tell Jasna about this new negotiating success. Her brother, too.

"So, where do you want to meet him?" Malone asked.

"How about the bar at Chez Jacques? Is that too small and closed-in?"

"No, small is good. We can get there beforehand and let the

maitre d' know what's going on. We'll be at your house shortly to get you wired up."

"What if Xander notices the wire?"

"He won't. Besides, we'll have our people sitting nearby."

Fifteen minutes later, standing in her kitchen, Iris felt all too conscious of the small plastic box taped to her back. It was hidden under an oversized sweater and wires ran under one arm to a mike hidden in her collar. In her mind she tried to work the questions Malone had given her into a natural-sounding conversation, but the flow of conversation would depend on whatever agenda Xander brought to the meeting. Did he want to confess to Iris that he had indeed taken Lara, and now felt contrite? Unlikely...

She decided to drive the nine blocks to Chez Jacques. Her Jeep might come in handy if she needed to make a hasty escape. Ellie, predictably, had tried to talk her out of taking this risk, regardless of what she felt about Jasna, and pointed out that wearing a wire for the police exceeded Iris' pay grade as an adjunct professor. Ellie was right, but Iris headed there anyway.

Showtime.

*　　*　　*

Chez Jacques had set up a heavy velvet curtain around the front door to protect the bar from the chilly drafts off the street. Iris pushed it aside and looked around the cheery, yellow-walled space. No sign of Xander. The maitre d' gestured Iris over to the only empty table, in a corner of the small front room. She glanced around at the lively bar scene wondering who else was in on the plan for her meeting.

She beckoned to the waiter, discreetly slipped him a twenty dollar bill, and instructed him to leave the alcohol out of whatever she ordered later. He gave her a wink and turned away just as Xander appeared through the curtain, entering like an actor walking on stage. His arm was in a sling and he held himself stiffly. As he approached to greet her with his usual kiss on each cheek, she drew back.

"What happened to you? You look like you've been inside a cement mixer! Were you in a fight?" she asked.

Xander sank heavily into a chair across from her. He had a black eye, a gash across his cheek, and probably more damage she couldn't see, judging by the way he walked.

"A one-sided fight. Lara's father thought that I might be the villain who took her and that he might be able to beat some truth out of me."

Iris noticed that his left hand trembled slightly. "My God! Do the police know about this?"

"They're the ones who saved my life. I just got out of the hospital. I'm fine now, or they say I will be in a few days. I just don't want the press to find out about this. I don't need any more links to that girl."

Iris couldn't believe that Malone hadn't mentioned this development, but then realized he probably didn't want Iris to have revealed by her reaction that she may have had inside information. And Budge—she'd have to think of some way to forestall him from staking out the Malkin pool where Xander swam until his injuries were healed. He'd definitely want to write about the beating.

"Thank you for meeting me," Xander said. His eyes darted around the room. The waiter hurried over to take their drink order. Iris ordered a "vodka" tonic while Xander made the poor man recite the restaurant's entire selection of wines by the glass.

"How can I help?" Iris asked. She really did feel badly for him. He looked to be in a lot of pain.

After a pause, Xander spoke. "On Saturday morning you kindly offered to mention to the police"—here Xander seemed to straighten in his chair as if girding himself for something unpleasant—"that you had seen me on the evening that the girl, Lara, went missing."

Iris nodded. "But then you explained to the press that Lara may have discovered you were her biological father. So I thought

179

you wouldn't need my alibi."

"It seems now that someone is trying to implicate me in her disappearance."

"What do you mean? Who?"

"That's the problem. I don't know." He looked around for his drink.

No sooner were the glasses set down than Xander took a quick gulp of his white Burgundy, then continued. "There have been some developments that may have given the police a mistaken impression about me. My solicitor thinks it might be helpful if you would let them know that you saw me at home that night."

"But if I come up with an alibi now, won't that just draw more attention to you? Maybe you're overreacting." Iris sipped her tonic water. "What makes you think someone is trying to set you up?"

"I just know," Xander said, a bit too loudly, then looked embarassed at his outburst.

"I'm not trying to be difficult," Iris said. "It's just that if I'm going to get involved, I really need to understand what's going on." She was trying to set up the dialogue Malone had given her.

Xander rested his head in his hands."I'm going to have to tell you something. In confidence." When he looked up at her, he looked defeated. Even the blue of his eyes had dimmed. "When my house was broken into it looked as if nothing had been taken." He paused.

"But something had been?" Iris coaxed.

"I think my computer password was discovered in the study. I always have to write it down because Nils is always changing it. Someone used my password to open my laptop account and install pornography."

Iris cocked her head. "Why would anyone do that?"

He pursed his lips and seemed to be counting to ten. "Certain pornography sites are monitored by the government to track down the people who visit them."

Iris leaned forward and whispered, "Wouldn't that add up to most of the male population?"

Xander allowed himself a slight smile. "It wasn't regular pornography. It involved young girls."

"Oh. Like Lara."

"As you say," he bowed his head. "That action combined with someone sending her to my office makes me look involved in her disappearance, don't you see?"

She did see. And Xander probably didn't even know yet about the keys to the blue van being found in his house. It had always been Iris' fate to see things clearly from everyone else's perspective. "But who would hate you so much? You would know if you had an enemy like this."

"I don't know who's behind this. I just know that I need to try to protect myself." He surprised her by reaching across the table and taking her hand. "Iris, will you help me?"

Iris drew back but said nothing. What if Xander was telling the truth? What if he was a victim, too?

"I think the police searched my house today." Xander leveled at Iris the most pain-filled look she had ever seen. It was full of more desperation than his words could convey. He finished simply with, "Will you help me?"

She met his eyes, feeling like a Judas even as she told the truth. "Yes, I'll tell the police what I saw."

CHAPTER 38

In the nightmare, Iris found herself wrapped in a dank bedspread, shackled by one leg to a wall. It was dark in the room but a sliver of light penetrated through a dusty window. Her throat felt sore. She must have been screaming for a long time. Her ankle was chafed raw and her empty stomach ached with hunger. Had she been left here to die slowly of starvation?

Edging crablike over to the wall, she wrapped both hands on the chain near to the ring and yanked a few times, shoving with her legs as hard as she could.

She scrabbled back away from the wall and tried pulling again, but there was no solid place to plant her feet. A stab of pain shot up her leg as a splinter of wood jabbed her bare foot. Trapped in the dark, she pounded her fists against the floor in frustration.

She curled up in a fetal position, cocooned in the bedspread, and tried to drift off to sleep when the whirr of a car's engine outside snapped her into awareness. The car stopped nearby, its door clicked open, and then slammed. Iris heard keys scraping in a lock. Heavy footsteps sounded, moving up inside the building. She couldn't stop herself shaking. She realized that there were worse ways to die than starvation. She had no doubt that this intruder was there to violate her, to hurt her in unspeakable ways that would make her eventual death seem like a relief.

Iris screamed as loud as she could, but as she woke, she heard only the tiniest of strangled-sounding pleas: "Help me, please help me."

She sat bolt upright in her bed, breathing hard, her heart thundering. With both hands she touched her chest to feel if it was literally jumping out of her chest. Sheba sat next to her on the bed, whimpering, trembling. She stroked the dog.

Iris felt the nightmare trying to tug her back. "It's not real," she repeated again and again.

She turned on her reading light and waited for the dream to recede as she blinked her eyes and her bedroom came into focus.

Maybe this was what Lara was experiencing right now— abject terror. And if the police were only focused on Xander, and he hadn't taken her, then they would never be able to find Lara in time.

CHAPTER 39

The following morning Russo watched Malone standing before the murder board, studying a map. Malone pulled a small piece of paper from his pocket, consulted it, adjusted the calipers on his compass, and drew a large circle around the city of Cambridge.

Russo cleared his throat. "I tracked down Crazy-dog, the guy the professor saved in Bosnia."

"Yes?"

"His name is Nils Jensen, an architect from Holland. He's thirty-eight, a little younger than DeWitt. We knew he worked in DeWitt's Amsterdam office, but get this: he's here in Cambridge acting as DeWitt's teaching assistant. He also goes back and forth to Europe to bring things from the office."

"Is Jensen here now?"

"His plane lands a little after one this afternoon."

"Bring him in for an interview," Malone said.

"I'll send someone to meet him at the airport, catch him before he can speak with DeWitt. By the way, on the tape last night, how did DeWitt know we'd already searched his house?"

"How do I know? The guy seems totally anal. We probably didn't line his boots back up precisely enough. In any case, he's on his guard. Foster said he didn't budge from his house either before or after the meeting with our Ms. Reid at the restaurant."

"Seems like the tape from last night isn't going to do us much good."

"I told the D.A. about the girl's visit to DeWitt's office and his lie about the van. I told her about the Feebs finding kiddie porn on his computer. She says we need more solid evidence linking him to the girl— DNA, fibers. You heard what DeWitt said to the Reid woman. He's going to say that someone's framing him. Even Ms. Reid seemed to be on the fence about his guilt by the end of their conversation. Of course it didn't help that he showed up looking like he'd just gone five rounds with Muhammad Ali."

Malone's voice was tinged with irritation, big time. Russo knew that he had missed his Tuesday night AA meeting to stake out the rendezvous. He'd exchanged a 'get out of jail free' card to the Sidran woman for getting DeWitt to speak on tape, and he still he had nothing actionable to show for it.

Russo tipped his bald head toward the map. "Think we can narrow down the search zone?"

Malone deliberately traced the wide circle with his finger. "This is the furthest distance the van could have gone in two roundtrips given the distance on its odometer."

"How do you know he only made two roundtrips?"

"I don't. But I figure that's the minimum he could've made. First, to scope out the hidey hole and second, to drop her off. If he's used the van for more trips, he's still inside this circle. This is the farthest he could have gone."

"That's a lot of territory to cover. It even crosses the New Hampshire border, up by Manchester."

"Yeah. We're going to have to reach out to all the local agencies. We should also find out if our friend Jensen ever rents vehicles. Maybe has a zipcar account. He could be in on this thing with DeWitt. If they're using zipcars to get around, that would completely mess up the map which I've based on the van's milage. Still, what else can we do but start with some assumptions. Got any better ideas?"

They could hear Malone's phone ringing from inside his office and they both hurried toward it.

Malone slid into his desk chair then lifted the receiver.

Russo listened impatiently to one side of the conversation

from the doorway.

"Yeah, I understand it's only preliminary," Malone said. "What did you get off them?"

Russo approached, trying to get his ear closer to the receiver. Malone elbowed him off.

"You're sure? OK, thanks."

Malone hung up and looked grimly at his partner. "Human blood on the boots."

CHAPTER 40

O n Wednesday morning Iris opened her copy of the *Globe* to
see, as expected, Budge's front page article about everything
that had really happened on the night of Lara's disappearance. He
referred to Jasna as "an unnamed friend" and made it sound as if
Lara had stopped by Jasna's apartment while running away from
her father, and had gotten kidnapped while the "friend" was out.
Budge avoided making it sound as if Jasna was helping Lara run
away. Iris owed him thanks for that at least. She wondered, though,
why the article hadn't mentioned the suspicious blue van or
Xander's connection to it. The police had probably made Budge
put a freeze on that part of the story.

Iris already had a message in to Budge saying she'd learned
that DeWitt had pulled a muscle, so wouldn't be swimming for
awhile but wasn't it good that, thanks to her, he was able to write
that front page article about what had actually happened on the day
Lara disappeared. Hopefully he would consider all her debts paid.

Iris' phone buzzed. "Hi, Ellie," she said noting the caller I.D. "I survived my first wearing-a-wire experience."

"Let's hope it's your last. So, what did Xander have to say?"

"First of all, he'd been beaten up by Lara's barbaric father. He had to spend the night in the hospital."

"That's terrible. Is Xander ok? I knew that the father was a brute. His eyes are too close together."

"Very scientific. Xander should be ok in a few days. But the reason he wanted to meet was to tell me he thinks someone's setting him up. He said that after his house was broken into, he found porn on his computer. Young girl porn. I have to admit he sounded pretty convincing."

"Maybe he downloaded it himself and now that he's being scrutinized by the police he needs to explain how it got there. Did he explain why he lied about having access to the van?"

"Detective Malone didn't want me to bring that up. They're still hoping Xander will lead them to wherever he's hidden Lara. But here's the thing— I'm not so sure anymore that he's the one who took her."

"Why not?"

"If you had seen the misery in the guy's eyes, you'd question too whether he could be the kidnapper."

"But let's think about his possible agenda—why did he want to tell you about this alleged set-up?" Ellie asked.

"He wanted me to alibi him to the police for that night."

"Did you agree?"

"Yes, I could say in full honesty that I would tell the police what I saw that night."

"Our architect superstar sounds a bit paranoid."

"On the other hand, he's got so much to lose by getting caught up in a scandal. What if someone really is framing him and the police are zeroing in on the wrong guy? Last night, I had a terrifying nightmare about Lara. It made me want even more for the poor girl to be safe, and for the police to lock up whichever monster took her."

"Amen." There was silence on the line, then Ellie said, "I saw Luc yesterday."

"Oh?"

"He was crossing Mass Ave toward the Paradise and didn't see me."

"Did he look like he hadn't been sleeping? He gets these deep shadows under his eyes."

"He looked pretty haggard." Ellie said. "How are you doing?"

"I have to stop myself from calling him twenty times a day."

"Maybe you *should* call him and see what he has to say. You guys are good together. I can't believe that he doesn't have an explanation for this."

"Whatever the explanation is, he should have told me four months ago."

"Don't let your pride get in the way here. Life isn't black or white. It's complicated sometimes."

CHAPTER 41

The man sitting in the interview room stroked his goatee nervously and stole the occasional glance at his watch. A messenger bag and rolling suitcase rested on the floor.

Russo sat shoulder to shoulder by Malone, studying DeWitt's assistant on the other side of the half-silvered mirror.

"Long enough?" Russo said.

"Let's find out."

They strolled into the adjoining room. Russo flipped the wall switch to start the recording system and listened to Malone start with the basics.

"My name is Nils Jensen. I live at Binnengasthuisstraat 27, Amsterdam, the Netherlands. I work as an architect for Co-op dWa. I am in Cambridge assisting Professor DeWitt with teaching a studio at Harvard GSD and keeping him up to date with office matters."

Nils' voice was high and raspy. His albino-fair hair, held

back in a pony-tail, and his slender frame gave him a feminine look.

"We've asked you here, Mr. Jensen, to see if you can help us understand some of the particulars of Professor DeWitt's life here in Cambridge."

Nil's eyes darted between the two detectives. "Have you asked Professor DeWitt your questions? Why are you asking me?"

"We know how it works with these big honchos." Malone said. "The assistant is the one who does all the work behind the scenes—am I right? Putting together slides for his talks, organizing his schedule, setting up his living arrangements. You probably even buy his coffee and cereal, don't you?"

"Yes, of course I do those things. The professor is a busy man. His favorite muesli and coffee must be carried here from Amsterdam in my luggage. He wouldn't have a clue how to shop in an American grocery store. But I don't understand why you want to know about this."

Malone paused a moment and replied thoughtfully, "That's right—the professor is a busy man. We don't want to disturb him if you can answer some simple questions for us. Then you can be on your way and we won't have to interrupt the professor's work. For example, can you tell us what his teaching schedule is?"

Russo noted how artfully Malone walked the assistant through twenty minutes of innocuous questions until Nils Jensen finally lowered his shoulders and relaxed back into his chair. Then Malone threw the ball to Russo. "Anything else?"

Russo appeared to think for a minute then asked, "How does the professor get around?"

Nils smiled indulgently. "He has a bicycle. That is how we Europeans navigate around our cities. Not everyone needs a car."

Russo continued, "But what if he needs to get out of the city? Do you ever rent cars for him, or does he maybe borrow a car from a friend?"

"No, I don't think he has needed a car since he's been here." Nils appeared to ponder the question. "No, wait. I did rent us a Zipcar when we went up to New Hampshire a few weeks ago. The professor wanted to see Frank Lloyd Wright's Zimmerman House. It was a Saturday when he wasn't teaching."

Russo jotted down a quick note to check on Zipcar accounts under Jensen's name, then asked, "Where is this Zimmerman house located?"

Nils frowned. "It didn't take too long to drive there, an hour or so. I did the driving of course. We went up in the morning and had lunch at a diner nearby. The diner had a tree in its name, I remember. I think the town is called Manchester—does that sound right?"

"Yes," said Malone, the corners of his mouth turning up. "That sounds just right."

CHAPTER 42

Iris had come to Jasna's desk at GSD during studio time, ostensibly to give her a desk crit, only to find her student visibly unsettled.

"The police came to my apartment and dragged me down to the station house. It took forever to get out. You said that I wouldn't get into trouble." Since Sunday, Jasna's eyes had become enormous and her body looked even more shrunken than usual. Her oversized sweater and leggings made her look like a child.

"You're not in trouble. I don't want you to worry. The important thing is that the police now know all the relevant information so they can track down Lara. I sent my brother to make sure you were all right. Did he explain that no charges are going to be filed against you? That *Globe* reporter is also going to keep your name out of the story."

Jasna looked at her skeptically.

"It's out of our hands, Jasna. The police are the ones

equipped to follow the leads," Iris said. "Now I need you to focus back on your schoolwork. I understand how worried you've been, but this master's program requires students to work night and day. You don't want to get an incomplete and jeopardize your student visa. The final jury is in a little more than a month and your project is way behind. You can catch up, but you need to put your full attention on it. And remember what I said about cutting yourself. You should go to Harvard Health and see what they can do to help."

Iris touched the girl's shoulder to reassure her. Jasna flinched.

"It looks like your project hasn't progressed since last Friday's crit. Why don't you spend your studio time today working on your model. I can meet with you tomorrow afternoon to have a look at it, okay?"

With a parting smile that she hoped conveyed some confidence that all would turn out well, Iris headed for the open stairway to the level above, then turned through the door from the airy, skylit studios into the hard, heavy concrete side of the building.

As she approached Xander's office, ready to reassure yet another person about her efforts on their behalf, she heard raised voices through the slightly open door.

"First you get beat up. Then the police search your house. You said you had everything under control."

"How was I supposed to know that maniac was lying in wait for me?" Iris heard a scraping sound. "Wait, Nils."

"Let go of my arm. I can't believe you told that Reid woman about the porn on your computer. You should have discussed it with me first."

"I explained that it was planted. I could tell that she felt sympathetic, and I need people on my side. She's my alibi for that night."

"Lucky she couldn't tell what you were really doing when she spied on you."

"Don't be vulgar. I was just listening to my Nabokov CD."

"By the way, you'd better get rid of that."

"They've already searched. Besides, those Keystone cops wouldn't know the plot of a Nabokov book if it were spelled out in one-syllable words."

"Don't be so arrogant. They're not idiots. They were actually pretty clever at getting me to tell them that you rent Zipcars to get around."

"It happens to be the truth."

"So, you're sure the Reid woman will tell the police she saw you?"

"When has my charm ever failed to work? You're the one who told me to cultivate a relationship with a woman during this Harvard semester, and it's turning out to be helpful."

"I hope you didn't have to put too much effort into it."

"Luckily, I could tell she wasn't interested in getting between the sheets with me. I do have my limits."

Iris tiptoed away from the door, shock making her numb. She stumbled the rest of the way down the corridor, the sound of their chuckling dying out behind her.

CHAPTER 43

By Wednesday afternoon at four, Russo sat across from Malone in a booth, studying the illustrated menu at the Oak Tree Diner in Manchester, New Hampshire. Framed photos of satisfied patrons, dating back decades, smiled down from the walls.

"This is the place where Jensen said they stopped after seeing the Frank Lloyd Wright house," Russo said, then looked up. "Do you think the locals are going to take the search seriously?"

"Would you?" Malone answered. "We're asking them to find a needle in a haystack. Lara's been gone a week. We only have circumstantial evidence that DeWitt took her. We know that he came up here a few weeks ago and that the van's odometer supports two additional roundtrips. You saw Sergeant Ruiz's face when we told him what we have."

"But this is a twelve-year-old girl. They have to take it seriously... on the off-chance... " Russo trailed off.

"It's not like this city doesn't have their share of locally-sourced crime. But Ruiz seemed like a decent guy. I'm sure he'll make an effort."

A middle-aged waitress with a tight perm and a black apron over her blue jeans approached their booth. "You gentlemen know what you'd like?"

After reading her name tag Malone asked, "What do you recommend, Trudy?"

"The chili's good today, but the Canadian pork pie is our house specialty. Comes with two eggs and hash browns."

They ordered one of each.

Ten minutes later Russo devoured the pie and the eggs and the potatoes without interruption while Malone tucked into a huge mug of chili slathered in melted cheese.

They pushed away their plates just as Trudy returned to hand them back their pair of menus. "How about some strawberry shortcake or chocolate eclairs for dessert?" She pointed her pencil at the glass-front refrigerator behind her. "With coffee?"

Knowing his partner's weakness for chocolate, Malone said, "Two eclairs with coffee, black." Then, as he handed back his menu, he asked, "Would you happen to know if there are any empty buildings around here? Properties for sale or maybe some place that's abandoned?"

Trudy arched a brow. "You guys looking for a weekend place—a fixer-upper?"

"No," Malone answered a bit too emphatically. "We're police. Looking for a missing girl. We think she might be hidden somewhere around here. Maybe some place visible from the street between here and the highway."

Trudy looked shocked. "Oh, my word. Let me ask the cook. I'll be right back."

They could see the two conferring animatedly as Trudy parceled their desserts onto plates. After distributing the eclairs, the waitress explained, "We don't really have many empty buildings around here, but Frank reminded me that last summer some Boston folks built a vacation home nearby. They came in here to eat whenever they drove up to check on the progress. Frank says there's an old barn where the workers stored their tools. His cousin worked on the crew and claims his hammer was stolen from that barn— his favorite framing hammer. I guess they'll tear down the barn now that the house is done. May have already done it, for all I know."

"Have the owners moved in yet?" Malone asked.

"Like I said, it's a summer place. The contractor finished the house last month, but I guess the owners are waiting to move in 'til next year. I haven't seen them in awhile."

Trudy refilled their coffee cups with cool precision from an impressive height. Malone and Russo got her to sketch a map to the property on a napkin before she retreated to tally up their check.

They left her a large tip.

It was not difficult for the detectives to spot the freshly-shingled house and weathered barn from the road. Perhaps DeWitt had been drawn over for a closer look at the house's graceful modern form.

Russo steered the Ford into the driveway and cut the engine. No lights were on in the house. The late afternoon shadows provided the men some camouflage as they approached the dilapidated outbuilding on foot, Glocks out at the ready, avoiding the main path. Patches of red paint clung to the structure but otherwise it was pretty much as brown as the mud around it.

Malone signaled for Russo to watch the main door while he disappeared around the side. Russo squinted through a broken window. The interior looked and sounded deserted. He caught the acrid smell of manure, but the barn probably hadn't housed animals in many years. He could see some construction trash on the floor— nail coils, crushed cardboard boxes, along with a few abandoned soda cans. Malone returned to Russo's side and signaled. They gave up any hope of surprise as the heavy door swung open, creaking loudly on its tired hinges.

They took out flashlights and went separately into the gloom. It was colder inside than out. Russo tried to ignore the musty odor rising from the rough floorboards. He considered climbing up a wooden ladder to the hay loft, but doubted the rungs would hold his weight.

Russo heard Malone's steps behind him and turned in time to see his lieutenant trip over an old wooden trough. Malone reached out his hands to break the fall.

Russo came running to help.

"Don't come any closer," Malone called out to him. "There's blood here. A lot of blood."

CHAPTER 44

After their discovery Russo and Malone got booties and gloves from the field kit in the Ford, but the damage was done.

As they waited for Sergeant Ruiz and his team to arrive, they inspected the rest of the barn to make sure they hadn't overlooked the source of the gore. They found a flowered bedspread crumpled in a dark corner and a section of frayed rope next to the wooden trough. The blood had turned brown but still gave off a sweet, coppery smell.

Russo set down a lantern near the bedspread and fumbled in his pocket.

"What are you doing? Don't mess up the crime scene," Malone said.

"The bedspread matches the description the Sidran woman gave," Russo said. "I thought we should have a photograph to show her for confirmation."

"Okay, but do it now before the scene gets turned over to Ruiz. After that we'll be getting all our information second-hand," Malone said.

Ten minutes later, several crime scene technicians, already suited up in plastic coveralls, filed into the barn. Ruiz followed with an exhausted look that signaled it was the end of his shift. He caught sight of the bloody trough and sucked air in through his teeth as he noted the smear mark running through the blood.

"That your palm, Malone?"

Malone's ears turned pink.

"Sorry. I tripped."

"How'd you ever find this place?" Ruiz asked. "You must have been holding back when you briefed me back at the station."

"The waitress at the Oak Tree Diner gave us a tip and it panned out." Malone said. "Mind if we hang around?"

"Show your I.D.s to the uniform out by the tape, then stay out of the way."

As they watched from the sidelines, Malone kept up a running dialogue in Connor's ear concerning his interpretation of the blood spatter—speculating whether the victim had been dragged or bludgeoned or shot.

Russo half listened and fought the urge to retch as he

imagined what the girl might have gone through. After he'd put down his camera, the scene had become more real for him.

"Note the medium-sized droplets and the elliptical tail over there," Malone said.

Russo was more interested in watching a forensic tech scrape some of the blood into a collection tube, then squeeze several droplets onto a test bar. After a few minutes the tech announced to Ruiz, "Two red lines. Human blood."

"What's the girl's blood type?" Ruiz asked Malone.

"A positive."

"We'll put a rush on the labwork and let you know," Ruiz said.

After setting up an array of powerful lights, a photographer meticulously documented the trough from all angles, followed by evidence techs who sealed the remaining blood into polythene bags. Then they carefully wrapped the bedspread and rope in paper, which were then bagged and tagged. Other crime scene techs dusted for prints and inspected every surface for possible clues.

Through the open barn door, Russo could see the snout of a van pull up in the featureless, gray light. Its doors rolled open, then slammed. Russo could hear excited yelping and whining. He knew that the dogs were eager to scour the nearby woods for a body, perhaps not yet fully cold. Assuming it really was Lara's blood, and the presence of the bedspread gave that high odds, their missing person investigation might have just turned into a homicide case.

Malone followed Ruiz outside to watch the dogs do a quadrant search, but Russo's attention followed a crouching female tech shining her flashlight at an angle to the dirt floor near the trough. She took a black box and a flat grounding plate out of her field kit and lay mylar film over the area she'd been inspecting. Russo had heard about electrostatic dust print lifters but never seen one in action. The tech placed the box to overlap the mylar and the plate, then punched the box's "on" button. She passed a rubber roller over the mylar. Russo moved closer, mesmerized, as an image materialized.

He rushed outside to find Malone. Following the sounds of footsteps and breaking branches, he threaded his way through the densely packed evergreens before spotting Malone's tall, lanky sillouette.

"Malone," Russo shouted, "you've gotta see. We got a footprint."

CHAPTER 45

As Iris was clearing her dinner plate, she heard a TV reporter's voice announcing a breaking development in the Lara Kurjak case. She hurried to her living room and stood in front of the screen, watching images of people in coveralls hauling mysterious plastic bags out of an old, tilting barn surrounded by sawhorse barriers and crime scene tape. *Manchester, New Hampshire Crime Scene* scrolled across the bottom banner.

A field reporter, lips pursed but eyes wild with suppressed excitement, led with a "shocking" discovery. "The Manchester police are saying that they have found evidence in this barn that appears to be linked to Lara Kurjak's alleged abduction from a friend's apartment in Cambridge."

The screen shifted to a bland-looking anchorman sitting calmly in the studio. A disembodied voice said, "Chuck, do we know yet whether the police have found the girl?"

There was a time delay as Chuck clutched his earpiece. "No,

211

Bob. I overheard some technicians talking about collecting blood samples, but there's been no sign of a body yet. The police have been searching the barn and these woods behind me for the girl."

The camera obligingly panned the woods behind him.

"Are the dogs helping with the search, Chuck?"

The camera zoomed in on a police handler directing three panting German Shepherds into a van. Iris recognized Lieutenant Malone in the shadow of the van, staring stoically ahead.

"That's right, Bob. These hard-working K-9s have been combing the woods for the last two hours without any success. But Segeant Emilio Ruiz, of the Manchester Police, assures me that the search will continue."

Bob wrapped up with, "This is the first major break in the Kurjak kidnapping. We will keep you updated on any developments in the case."

Iris switched off the TV and sank into the sofa. Lara must be dead. That poor, poor girl. She must have been taken to this barn in New Hampshire, and then... Iris hugged a pillow as a tear rolled down her cheek. Sheba jumped up onto the sofa and nestled in with her.

Could Xander have possibly done this? After what she'd

overheard him saying in his office, she had no trouble believing that he used people to get whatever he wanted. She'd felt so humiliated by how he'd spoken about her with Nils that she hadn't even told Ellie all of his hurtful words. But kidnapping, raping and murdering a twelve-year-old girl? Hadn't the police been watching him? Or had he done it on that first night? Still, she couldn't reconcile her memory of Xander sitting peacefully in his living room in his silk pajamas with the scene of this bloody barn.

Then again, Nils could have taken Lara. They could be in this together. Did pedophiles work in pairs?

But why did Xander say it was true that he had to rent Zipcars to get around? That implied that someone had planted the key to the neighbor's van in Xander's house. And if that was true, then Xander's claim of being set up might also be true.

He had so much at stake. If any credible trail led from Xander to this bloody New Hampshire barn, his life's work would be over. Even if he were able to somehow defend himself, even if a malicious setup could eventually be proved, at the end of the day, he would be forever linked to this scandal.

She was going to have to tell Detective Malone what she'd overheard. It was too hard for her to separate her newfound dislike for Xander DeWitt from any rational analysis of the facts. Besides, it was his job to solve Lara's disappearance. She imagined that she could leave out some parts of what Xander had said.

CHAPTER 46

Xander clutched his side as he gingerly squatted down to scoop up his copy of the Thursday *Boston Globe* from the front porch. His broken rib ached fiercely and his shoulder still sent out sharp jabs of pain at random moments. Thank God that Neanderthal, Kurjak, would be locked up at least for the remainder of Xander's time here in the States.

He poured his first coffee of the day from the stovetop espresso maker and carried it to the marble table by the window. When he saw the *Globe* headline *Lara Kidnapping Tied to Barn in New Hampshire*, he dropped abruptly into a chair. He fumbled in a front pocket for his cigarette pack and shook one out. It took him three tries to light it.

He read the article carefully. It was written under the byline of William Buchanan, who seemed to be making the Lara story his personal ticket to the front page. These reporters were like vampires.

The police had found blood and other physical evidence, but no body, in a barn in Manchester, New Hampshire. Wasn't that the city where he and Nils had toured the Frank Lloyd Wright house several weeks before? His chest constricted.

The previous day Xander had grilled Nils on every word his assistant had said to the police. Nils had had the nerve to be annoyed with Xander for going offscript while Nils had been naïve enough to volunteer information to the police about their visit to New Hampshire.

"I figured I had to give them something," Nils had said. "What could be more innocent than our trip up to see that Wright house? It wasn't secret. You gave a presentation to the whole school the following week, featuring your many photos of the place."

Then Nils had added "I didn't tell them about any of the important things. I didn't mention Thailand."

The mention of Thailand struck Xander with a frisson of dread, but also of excitement. His stress level was so high. God knew he needed something to look forward to. Just then was when he had made the mistake of asking Nils if he had settled all the details for Xander's Christmas trip to Thailand. Nervously looking around the room, Nils had reminded Xander that he was under serious scrutiny by the police as well as the Pritzker prize committee. Any whiff of a scandal could prove disastrous. Xander could not go to Thailand in the foreseeable future.

"You're not the only one under suspicion. I've been covering up for you. If you go down, I go down," he'd said before huffing out of Xander's Harvard office. Since then, Nils hadn't responded to any of Xander's e-mails or phone calls.

Terrified at the prospect of a figurative noose tightening around his neck, yet filled with despair at missing out on his customary Christmas trip to Maurice's place in Chiang Mai, Xander thought back to the lovely Sumalee from last Easter. Her long perfect legs, and the sweet way she attended to his many needs.

What would Nietzsche do? he asked himself, as he always did at an important juncture. *He would probably call his solicitor.*

CHAPTER 47

Iris should have gone to see Jasna the previous night, after she watched the TV news. Her poor student was probably beside herself with guilt after the New Hampshire barn report. Jasna had already been in a fragile state, and this might have put her over the edge. Iris hoped the girl hadn't done anything drastic.

As she walked along her usual route to the GSD, her cell phone rang. Fishing it out of the depths of her purse, she saw that it was Sterling and answered the call.

"It looks like your crazy scheme to shield the Sidran woman has panned out," he said. "The D.A. has officially dropped the charges against her. Seems the case is finally going somewhere despite her obstruction. Listen, Iris, how convinced are you that this professor friend of yours isn't a pedophile, and maybe even capable of kidnapping and murder?"

Iris felt her annoyance level start to escalate. "He's not my friend. I have no idea what his morals are like. He claims he's being set up, which, if true, makes me worry that the police might be looking in the wrong place. My fear is that Lara will be found too late, dead, and that my student will be devastated by her role in it."

"Take some advice from your attorney. You've already done your good deed by keeping this student from getting the book thrown at her. Now put some distance between yourself and this DeWitt fellow. I think he's going to be arrested soon. If you become his alibi, you're probably going to get caught up in the court case, and you could be seriously tainted if he goes down for this crime."

"But I already told the police what I saw. I don't want to be involved in a court case that could drag on for months."

"You're the one who's been cozying up to the police without consulting your attorney first... I've got to go— another call's coming in."

Iris put away her phone and walked in through the heavy front doors of the GSD. Sterling's phone call had solidified her decision not to call Detective Malone after all. She would not tell him what she'd overheard the day before. None of it had been new information, beyond the fact that Xander had been using her friendship as a front. Maybe he was gay, who knew? But why would that produce any stigma in this day and age, and within their professional and academic circles?

She climbed the open metal steps to her studio level, trying to put aside her own concerns so she could concentrate on what must be going on for Jasna.

But, as she approached the narrow opening to Jasna's desk pod, she heard giggling. A man's head turned toward her and she recognized Rory, slouched on Jasna's second desk. His grin faded just as Jasna playfully shot back at him, "In your dreams, Mister Alsop."

"Hi, Iris. Ahh... I'd better get back to work," Rory said, slipping out as Iris moved into the disordered work area. It looked like Jasna was finally spending some serious time here.

Jasna's expression collapsed into sadness when she saw Iris. Her voice became low. "The police came by this morning and showed me a picture of the bedspread they found. I told them it was mine. It had blood on it. Lara must be dead and it's all my fault. I'll never forgive myself."

Iris rested her hand lightly on Jasna's arm. "It's not your fault. The police will find whoever took her. You need to put this out of your mind. I know it's hard, but you need to try."

Jasna stared down at her desk. "I've been up all night working on this model, while Lara's body might be..." She turned silently away.

"Let me have a look at your model then." Iris crouched to put her eye level with the model.

Iris took a long deep breath and examined the model from all angles, studying the various facades as they related to the volumes of the building. "You've gotten a lot done. It really captures your idea of inward focus, and I think it's starting to express that theme on the exterior too. It's well executed. You did good work, especially considering that it included pulling an all-nighter."

"Thank you," Jasna said, dully.

After more design encouragement and pointed pleas to check in with Harvard Health, Iris left her, but she couldn't get out of her head the sound of Jasna's carefree giggling with Rory. What made this girl tick?

CHAPTER 48

They were finally making progress on the case, just not the good kind of progress. Russo was skimming through a pile of reports on his desk that Thursday morning, trying to forget the image from the previous evening of Ivano Kurjak's face dissolving into tears of despair. He had drawn the short straw so it was his job to drive out to MCI, the men's correctional facility out in Concord, to notify the father about their findings in New Hampshire, while Malone had gone to get a search warrant for the boots they had taken dirt samples from at DeWitt's house.

A definite DNA match of the blood might take weeks to confirm, but the discovery of Jasna's bedspread made it appropriate to give her father an update, even if he was serving time for assault and battery. The medical examiner's initial opinion was that an eighty-pound girl would be hard-pressed to survive the amount of blood loss left behind in the barn.

Russo rubbed his hand back and forth over his bald head as

223

was his usual nervous habit. He hadn't expected a guy who'd planned to marry his pre-teen daughter off to a complete stranger to show so much emotion.

He read through the follow-up interview with the man who had witnessed the blue van's departure from the Sidran woman's apartment building. The young father, a math graduate student at M.I.T., turned out to have a photographic memory for numbers, no great surprise. He'd even remembered the color of the *B, B & N* sticker from a Cambridge private school on the van's left rear window. Too bad he hadn't gotten a good look at the driver, or been there earlier when, presumably, the rolled-up bedspread was carried out.

As he flipped to a report from the van's forensic techs, Russo's eyes zeroed in on a high-lighted passage. "A small gold locket containing a photo of a young woman was found wedged under the carpet in the cargo compartment." It sounded like Ivano Kurjak was in for another painful visit from the police.

Russo cracked his knuckles as he headed over to the murder board. Malone joined him before he could pick up the dry-erase marker. Overnight, the older detective had assumed the animated air of a hunter in pursuit of his prey.

"Looks like New Hampshire isn't going to get territorial on

us," Malone said. "They're willing to kick the case to us since we've got all the prelim work done."

As he studied Russo's additions to the board he said, "We've finally got the trail but it looks like it might be too late to save the girl."

"Poor kid." Russo fidgeted with the marker. "Is it going to be hard to convict the bastard without finding her body?"

"A body usually turns up sooner or later," Malone said. "Remember the Scott Peterson case? Guy tosses his pregnant wife in the ocean so he can run off with his masseuse? Eventually the body washed up. In any case, the 'no body' cases actually have a pretty high success rate if the circumstantial evidence is any good. So that's our job—to connect the dots. We already know DeWitt's going to claim that it's a frame-up."

"I can't believe the dogs didn't find her in the woods. It seems like the earth just swallowed the kid up whole."

"Just remember—the D.A. only has to prove his guilt beyond a reasonable doubt. If everything else points to DeWitt, then we don't need the body. But don't give up hope yet. We might still find her. The son of a bitch could be keeping her hidden somewhere." Malone said.

"I don't know what's worse—if he killed her right away or if he's keeping her alive." Russo's shoulders slumped. "If his lawyer

Susan Cory

claims a frame-up don't they have to pretty much prove that someone else did it?"

"Who can they pin it on? Jensen's been alibied by a bartender from the South End, and we have no trail at all coming from the father."

"What if it was some jealous architect who, I don't know, had a professional grudge?"

"You'd have to be ice cold to kill an innocent girl just to discredit a guy like DeWitt. But that's why we need to make this case crystal clear."

Malone's cell phone buzzed and he clamped it up to his ear. His eyes turned hard, then one side of his lips curved upward. After finishing the call he turned to Russo. "The dirt we got from that boot at DeWitt's house matches the dirt near the boot impression at the barn. If the impression matches DeWitt's actual boot —plus the wear pattern and the traces of blood, then our case may have just moved past a reasonable doubt."

226

CHAPTER 49

Iris entered their shared office at the GSD and gave Ellie a distracted look.

"Where have you been?" Ellie asked. "I need you to look over the seminar I planned to give about Colin Rowe's urban typologies."

Iris sank into her chair. "About that talk. Any chance you could give the talk this afternoon? We can change the crits to Friday."

"Why? What are you up to?" Ellie frowned at her. "Does this have anything to do with the news report about what the police found in New Hampshire?"

Iris stared out the window. "I couldn't stop thinking about it last night. Remember Xander's presentation about the Frank Lloyd Wright house with all those recent photos? The house is located in Manchester, very close to that barn. Why would he be so dumb as to give a presentation advertising the fact that he was near an intended crime scene?"

"Maybe he didn't know when he gave that talk that he would go back there. Maybe it was a panicked spur-of-the-moment kind of thing."

"It just doesn't seem to add up, how an intelligent guy like Xander would commit a crime. He wouldn't make obvious mistakes," Iris said. "I just want to make sure that the right guy gets found and punished, for Lara's sake."

Ellie looked long and hard at her friend. "Why is this your job, Iris? What can you do that the police aren't already doing?"

"Xander is the most self-controlled man I've ever met. He has so much to lose. If he ever were to give in to his impulses, wouldn't he do it in his own country where at least he'd know where to avoid notice and cover his tracks?"

"We can't understand how Xander's impulse control works. Just because something seems out of character doesn't mean he didn't do it. Anyway, the police won't charge him unless they have airtight evidence connecting him to the crime."

"Sometimes the police zero in on the wrong guy and get fixated on him while the real culprit gets away."

Ellie looked unconvinced. "I don't think you give the cops enough credit."

"While I was staring at the ceiling instead of sleeping last night I did come up with another possible suspect," Iris said, and paused... "Xander's assistant, Nils."

"That wispy guy? He couldn't even lift a bedspread, let alone one containing a girl."

"Skinny guys can be surprisingly strong. He could be in it with Xander or he could be setting his boss up. Maybe he's tired of being in the shadow of Mr. 'My-Life-Is-a-Work-of-Art.' Nils was in one of those New Hampshire photos, so they were together on that trip. And Xander said Nils deals with all his computer and internet issues, so he could have planted something incriminating on that hard drive."

"Wouldn't Xander tell the police if he had any suspicions?"

"Maybe he doesn't realize that the awkward puppy who follows him around may have grown some teeth." Iris rubbed her eyes. "Sterling thinks they're going to arrest Xander soon. If he is the one who killed Lara, I'd be the first to want to see him locked up. I just wish I didn't feel so skeptical."

Ellie studied her. "Why do I have a feeling you have some dangerous plan in mind to find out if it's Nils?"

"Because you know me pretty well. And my plan won't be dangerous if you help me. If you can give your talk today in the meeting alcove on the fourth level, you'll be able to look down from time to time to make sure that Nils is busy with Xander's studio on the third tray. With that creepy white-blond hair, he'll be hard to miss."

"And what will you be doing while I play lookout?"

"I can check his apartment to see if there's anything suspicious there."

"You're proposing to break in?"

"Why not? We architects know all the vulnerable points of entry in a building, right? You can text me if you see him leave the class."

"I know you're *capable* of pulling this off, but what about the *wisdom* of doing it?" Ellie crumpled one of the three empty Diet Coke cans lined up alongside her laptop. "You're going to do this whether I help or not, aren't you?"

Iris gave her a helpless look and Ellie continued, "I might as well try to keep you safe. But if I text you that Nils is leaving, you have to promise me you'll hightail it out of there immediately."

Iris crossed her heart.

CHAPTER 50

Iris nestled her jeep between trucks in the parking lot of a roofing supply house in Nils' Somerville neighborhood, ten minutes by car or bike from the GSD. As she set off for his street a couple of blocks away, she sensed that she was being watched. She spotted two elderly women in puffy parkas sitting on their front porch smoking while tracking her every move. Luckily, Nils' dead-end street was out of their range of vision.

The structure stood at the far end of a densely packed row of houses and small apartment buildings. The faculty directory listed his apartment as #1R which Iris judged to be the first floor rear unit. A quick circle of the building confirmed a two-unit-per-floor arrangement. She toyed with the direct approach, credit-carding her way in through the front entry, but as she was about to step onto the front path a first floor curtain twitched open and a man's face scowled out at her. She could hear the raucous sounds of a TV game show in the background and hoped it would hold his attention while she worked her way in from the rear.

Backtracking one house, she circled around to a weed-choked backyard to assess her options. Nils' building was a squat boxy structure, stuccoed by someone with no understanding of Massachusetts winters. Had Harvard found this apartment for him? Iris could find no merits in its architecture. But for her purposes, it featured just what she'd been hoping for—a sliding glass door.

She darted between the yards, trying to stay out of #1F's line of sight. When she was flattened against the back wall, she checked her cell phone for texts. Nothing. The coast was clear. She scanned the door. No contact wires or motion sensers. Shielding her eyes, she saw no movement inside. She tested the door, but the latch held firm. Nils had been careful to lock it but hadn't bothered to insert a rod in the track to brace it shut.

She took a Swiss army knife out of the pocket of her cargo pants and flicked open the blade. Jockeying the knife back and forth between the glass and the rubber gasket's edge she felt the glass shift slightly. She retrieved a small wood shim from another pocket and wedged it into the tiny opening. Using the side of her Swiss army knife, she whacked the shim further into the gap. Then she pointed the tip of the blade up under the latch and lifted, managing to raise the hook clear of the latch and slide the door open.

She stepped into the semi-darkness of Nils' living room and rested on the edge of a sofa, waiting for her heart to stop thudding. Then she began a systematic search, starting with a quick look around. Bedroom, bathroom, kitchen, living room. No serious hiding places or hidden safes. In the bathroom she found several joints in a box of Band-Aids in the medicine chest, but nothing that could lead to Lara.

Moving on to the bedroom, she found a lone silky jacket hung in the closet. She searched his bureau, even inside the pockets of his pants, but found only a dry-cleaning receipt and a wadded up Snickers wrapper. She felt self-conscious going through his underwear drawer, learning that he wore skimpy briefs, but she had to be thorough. She opened the top drawer of his bedside table and her hand hovered over a photograph. She angled it toward the light filtering through a window. It showed two men, dressed in military fatigues, standing on a hillside. The middle man was a much-younger Xander, stripped to the waist. His physique was surprisingly chiseled, Iris noted, with a butterfly tattoo stretched over a toned shoulder, hands resting on his hips. She could barely recognize the baby-faced soldier standing next to him as Nils.

Iris tried to make sense of the image. Xander had mentioned performing some military stint in Bosnia when he was trying to pass himself off as Lara's father. So Nils had been there too. She had assumed that Nils was much younger. Xander's forceful personality and sophistication added years to his persona while Nils' waif-like appearance and graduate school wardrobe subtracted them.

Under the photograph she found a page ripped out of a magazine. It featured a picture of a hip-looking Xander in a black leather jacket. Iris recognized the shot from an interview *Time* magazine had done several years before about a high-wattage residential skyscraper Xander had designed in lower Manhattan.

These two items were the only things in the drawer. She shoved the photograph into a pocket and left the magazine article behind. Nils would notice the picture missing, but he wouldn't be able to trace the theft to her.

Iris checked her watch. She'd been inside for twenty-five minutes. She moved quickly to the living room. Judging by several CDs on a shelf, he liked classic jazz. She found a few design books in a foreign language, presumably Dutch. She read titles in the bookshelf and slipped out a hardbound book of poetry. In the front of the book she saw Xander's name in his small precise handwriting. Had he given this book to Nils?

There were few other personal possessions, no framed

photos. In her concentration on the hunt, she almost missed the sound of the heavy front entry door slamming shut. She scanned the room for a place to hide and dove inside the hall closet just as a key scraped in the apartment's lock. Peeking through a sliver of opening, she watched Nils hoist his bike up onto wall hooks with ease. Maybe he was stronger than he looked.

He lifted the strap off his messenger bag and tossed it on the sofa. Then he froze. Iris tried to see what he was looking at but his glasses caught the sun's glare. Then she saw it. The book. She had left out the damn poetry book. What could she possibly say if he caught her in his closet?

He picked up the book and studied its cover. Opening it to an earmarked page, he stared at the words intently while Iris' mouth went dry. Looking puzzled, he returned the book to the shelf. While the tension in Iris' body made her muscles ache, he returned to the sofa and dumped a stack of mail out of his bag, then calmly sifted his way through the pile, tossing the junk mail on the floor. Next he pulled out his laptop and booted it up. He waded through e-mails and pecked out a few replies. She was just massaging a cramp in her leg when she heard it— an impossibly loud chirp coming from her pocket.

Nils cocked his head and stood up.

She felt blood rushing to her ears.

He turned in her direction.

He took a step toward the closet, then waited, listening.

The buzz of his own cell phone made them both jump. Iris watched Nils reach for it on the coffee table, turning away. He spoke loudly in a language Iris didn't recognize. The conversation became animated. She let out her breath as he wandered into the kitchen.

Iris carefully opened the closet door and tiptoed out of the apartment.

CHAPTER 51

What effect was this room supposed to have on him? Intimidation? Xander had been in this interrogation room at the Cambridge Police Station before and, as before, he was mystified by how someone could design such a bland space. Okay—the one-way mirror made him uneasy, not knowing who might be watching him, but the windows didn't even have bars on them. They were probably thick laminated glass.

"Professor DeWitt, did you hear me?" asked the tall, skinny policeman with the protruding ears and cold eyes, tapping a photo.

Xander's glance took in a bloody piece of flowered fabric and he wrinkled his nose. "I've never seen that item before."

His solicitor, James Farrington, Esquire, alert as a sparrow, sat on the edge of his vinyl chair waiting for cause to jump in and object. He was making notes on a yellow legal pad. He had told Xander on the drive over that this meeting's purpose was merely for them to discover what evidence the police might have.

Now the younger policeman, the one with the shaved head who looked like he lifted weights, pulled a pair of boots out of a paper bag. He set them on the metal table. "Do you recognize these?"

Farrington shot Xander a warning look but didn't object.

Xander pulled over a boot and examined it. "I can't be sure. I do own ones similar to these, as I'm sure many people do. They're from a company called L. Bean I think. My assistant bought them for me."

The beefy cop continued, "When was the last time you remember wearing yours?"

Xander threw up his hands in exasperation. "Detective, if I wore these boots to commit a crime, do you really think I would have kept them?"

"Please answer the question."

"I only wear them if I anticipate having to walk in mud or rain. I leave them inside by the kitchen door."

"And when was the last time you used them?"

Xander thought for a minute. "When I went to New Hampshire." He sensed the two policemen stiffen slightly, "In mid-September, to visit a Frank Lloyd Wright house with my assistant. We took many photos and I gave a talk about it at the GSD two weeks ago."

Then it was the skinny cop's turn to produce a small bag. He slid out a set of keys and placed them on the table. "You told us last week that you had no access to a vehicle, that your assistant rented Zipcars if you needed to travel outside of Cambridge. Do you recognize these keys?"

Xander studied the tacky Bulldog keyring. An adrenalin rush of fear surged through him.

Farrington whispered a few words to Xander before collecting his papers and standing up.

"This is a fishing expedition. If you aren't going to arrest my client, we're leaving."

Xander got up to follow him.

Skinny Cop gestured Xander back to his seat. "These boots with blood identified as Lara Kurjak's on their soles and the keys belonging to her kidnapper's van were both found in your house. Xander DeWitt, we are arresting you for suspicion of the abduction and murder of Lara Kurjak. You have the right to remain silent..."

Xander didn't hear the rest of the warning. His ears buzzed with static. He felt faint. He could see Farrington's lips moving but couldn't make out the words.

The two policemen and Farrington accompanied Xander

down to a sub-basement area where he had to empty his pockets into a plastic bag and hand it to an officer inside a cage. Before leaving him there, his solicitor assured Xander that he'd get him out on bail the next morning. That meant he had to survive the night in this place.

A uniformed guard fingerprinted him, took his mug shot and made him change into a hideous orange jumpsuit. They called it "being processed," like an animal being led to the slaughterhouse. When the guard led Xander through a series of heavy doors to a stark, claustrophobic cell, the dull clang of the heavy door closing was the sound of the prisoner being cut off from his former life.

He slumped on the edge of a metal cot, hands on his knees as he stared at the concrete floor, rage boiling up inside him. He had lost control of the situation. He had never thought about enemies before. He had never worried about stepping on toes. His focus had always been on his ascent, not on looking over his shoulder.

Xander tried to tamp down his emotions, his anger, to let his intellect rise to the fore. He sat up cross-legged on the cot, hands resting on his knees, eyes closed. He needed to focus on the evidence against him. He couldn't rely on these idiot police bureaucrats to figure out that someone had planted those boots.

They just wanted to close their case.

He took three deep breaths.

Okay, his neighbor had left him keys to his garage and van, but Xander had never intended to use them. The van was a stick shift and Xander could barely drive an automatic. Where had he even put the damn keys after his neighbor had pressed them into his hand? Xander hadn't mentioned the keys to anyone, not even Nils.

And the boots. He knew that he hadn't gotten anyone's blood on them. Someone must have broken into his house and stolen them. He scrolled through his stored memories to recall who he might have invited inside the Howland Street house. Nils of course. But it was out of the question that Nils would ever set him up. He had saved the man's life.

Gilles had dropped by to see how he was getting along in the beginning of the semester. Xander couldn't imagine why Gilles would harbor any ill will toward him. Gilles was the one who had invited Xander to come to Harvard to teach this fall. Maybe it was part of some elaborate revenge scheme. Maybe Gilles was in this with another architect who felt Xander had wronged him. He'd have to consider that angle.

The only other person who had crossed his threshold was Iris

241

Reid. She had peered in the window at him on that fateful night. That was creepy. Then she had barged into his kitchen the next weekend. Maybe she was angry that he hadn't made a pass at her. Or maybe she was exacting revenge on behalf of someone else. She seemed like a crusader. He had told her about the porn planted on his computer. After he got out on bail he would need to confront her.

But first he had to get through the night. He could hear rustling coming from the cell on his left and a guy muttering to himself from the right. Would they have heard of his supposed crime? He had learned from television shows that child rape and murder were considered heinous crimes even by hardened criminals. Would someone attack him... or worse? He'd heard about what happens in jails. Oh, God.

Xander lay down on his cot and curled up in a fetal position. He closed his eyes again to block out the harsh fluorescent glare on his orange jumpsuit.

CHAPTER 52

At eight-thirty the next morning, Ellie tapped on Iris' kitchen door. She carried a copy of Friday's *Globe* tucked under an arm.

"Are you still speaking to me after I almost got you caught?" Ellie said.

"You're officially dropped from my list of reliable lookouts," Iris sniffed.

"Please forgive me. As I said last night, Rory got me talking and by the time I checked on Nils, he'd disappeared." Ellie laid down her copy of the newspaper and stabbed her finger at the headline, **Harvard Prof Arrested!** "How do you think Budge found out about Xander?"

"Sterling says the police often leak information to spread their own agenda. After the discovery in New Hampshire, they'd probably given up hope of Xander leading them to Lara alive, so there was no reason to continue sitting on the information. Plus,

Susan Cory

Budge and I saw the police search his house and discover the van next door, so Budge might have stationed a *Globe* intern outside the station, waiting for the other shoe to drop."

"Are you still thinking Nils might have set Xander up?" Ellie said as she made herself a cappuccino from Iris' countertop machine, suspending the conversation for several long seconds while she noisily frothed the milk.

"I can't figure out what's going on between them. They seem to be in cahoots about something but, even though they didn't know I could hear them, they didn't talk about anything that might have tied them to Lara."

"Show me the photo you found in his apartment."

Iris retrieved it from the desk in her office and they studied it together.

"Nice abs," Ellie remarked.

"Definitely a beefcake shot. It was tucked in with an interview of Xander from *Time* magazine along with a second badass photo of Xander wearing a black leather jacket."

"I remember that picture. Where did you find them?"

"In Nils' bedside table."

"Really?"

"I know... Just one photo in the living room might be a *Band*

244

of Brothers thing. But two photos in his bedside table? Of your boss? Who you see every day?"

"I can't see Xander returning the emotion, can you?" Ellie said.

Iris tipped her head. "No, I didn't get a sense of love or lust or much of anything at all when Xander mentioned Nils. But I didn't get the sense that many people get through to Xander's heart. I wonder if his indifference might have turned Nil's feelings into a desire to get back at him. If Xander was a pedophile, and a girl could successfully win his affection when Nils could not, he might decide to kill the competition, while framing Xander in the process. Certainly Nils has the easiest access for setting Xander up."

"True," Ellie said, sipping her cappuccino. "But there's something bothering me about how Lara got drawn into this. By all accounts, she led a sheltered life. She went from her parochial school to helping at her father's shop in the afternoons. According to the papers, she wasn't allowed to have a cell phone or even a Facebook page. Her father set her laptop to the most restrictive parental controls, so presumably she wasn't lured out to meet someone over the internet. Does that mean that the kidnapper spotted her on the street at random?"

"Or maybe he saw her at her father's store."

"Is there any way to find out if Xander or Nils ever went there?"

"If either of them took Lara, they'd hardly volunteer that they ever shopped there. I'm sure the police showed the father a picture of Xander, at least."

Iris stared out her bay window at the yellow leaves beginning to pile up on her bluestone terrace.

"Whether Xander took Lara or not, the architectural world now knows that he's been accused of a crime. I noticed, in Budge's article, that Gilles at GSD didn't offer any supportive comments."

"On the contrary, I'd say he went out of his way to distance himself from his star professor," Ellie said as she carried her cup to the sink.

There was the scrabbling sound of toenails on tile hearth as Sheba emerged from her favorite spot inside the kitchen fireplace and stared up at Iris meaningfully.

"Looks like it's time for someone's walk." Ellie grabbed her jacket. "I'd better let you two go."

*   *   *

Twenty minutes later Iris and Sheba started out on the two-mile path around Fresh Pond, Cambridge's reservoir. Iris sifted through her thoughts as entertaining snippets of conversation floated by her from Cantabrigians passing along the wide footpath.

Two middle-aged women with arms pumping power-walked toward her. "My landscape architect wants to do a koi pond but..."

Sheba resisted Iris' tug on the leash as the dog intently sniffed a bush, apparently a popular one.

A squat, bearded man with a scholarly face sat on a bench and, leaning toward his companion, said in a bemused tone, "...my students seem to have made a computer avatar of me."

Iris unsnapped Sheba's leash as they approached the small, muddy pond where dogs were allowed to swim. Sheba waddled into the chilly water up to her belly, then promptly turned and waddled right back out. Iris gave her a tiny liver-flavored treat.

As they rejoined the main path circling the reservoir, two women in shorts jogged by, one calling out to the other, "I've become a vegan but, you know, I still eat lobster and bacon."

Iris' attention shifted to a copse of trees on a hill. At this midpoint in October, the trees were turning colors at different rates. A big maple looked like it had been overturned and dipped partly in red paint, remaining green on its bottom branches. Rather than the slow fade to brown witnessed in most other parts of the world, fall in New England was a constantly changing display of fiery, improbable colors.

She clipped Sheba's leash back on and guided the dog around a sweet-looking elderly couple. As she passed them she caught the woman's words, "... depraved Harvard professor deserves to rot in a cage."

Iris turned up the collar of her anorak against the blustery morning chill and thought of Ellie's question about how the kidnapper might have focused on Lara in the first place. Maybe he saw her riding home on her bike. Or doing an errand. Maybe he followed her and discovered where she lived.

But on the day that Lara was taken, the girl had done something out of her usual routine. She'd slipped out of her apartment while her father was away and had gone to Jasna's place. Unless the kidnapper had been stalking her that evening, he wouldn't have known to look for her there. As she followed this train of thought, Iris almost walked into the path of an oblivious cyclist.

"Hey, watch it!" the cyclist yelled at her. Always someone else's fault...

The kidnapper must have been stalking Lara for some time before she disappeared from Jasna's apartment.

Iris stopped short, unintentionally yanking Sheba by her leash. *So her alibi for Xander was valid after all because she had seen him at home alone when whoever took Lara must have been stalking the girl.*

CHAPTER 53

Iris gazed curiously around the waiting room of the offices of Farrington, Farrington and Rose. Someone had spent serious money on the interior finishes of this State Street law firm. She admired the bookmatched sheets of Honduras mahogany veneer on the walls. They were detailed with elegant crown molding and simple casings, avoiding the stuffy impression of traditional, over-elaborate millwork.

"Mr. Taylor will be right out."

"Thanks, but I specifically asked to see Mr. Farrington, Xander DeWitt's attorney," Iris said.

"Mr. Taylor is working with Mr. Farrington on the case. He can help you." The receptionist's impassive face turned back to her computer monitor, probably trolling on eBay.

Iris had raced through her Friday afternoon desk crits with her students, then taken the T to this downtown office. Now it looked like she was going to be fobbed off on an underling who might not have the brains or stature to pass her information up the line.

She stood up cautiously as a tall, handsome man in an expensive suit approached with an automatically outstretched hand.

"I'm Martin Taylor," said the non-underling. His handshake was firm, eye contact practiced. "I understand you have some information on the Xander DeWitt case that you might wish to share. Let's sit down in the conference room."

They walked down an Oriental-carpeted hallway to a small, elegant room lined with bookshelves. He gestured her toward a leather chair. She suddenly felt self-conscious about telling her story to this important and probably very busy man.

"My brother's an attorney. He's warned me not to get involved, but I feel, in good conscience, that I need to come forward with something I saw. It seems futile for me to tell this to the police now that they've arrested Professor DeWitt."

"You sound like a good citizen, Ms. Reid. You say your brother's an attorney?"

"Yes, Sterling Reid."

"You're Sterling's sister? We played squash the other day." Martin Taylor stretched back in his seat and pantomimed an overhead smash.

"His younger sister. Please, call me Iris."

"So, Iris, how do you know Professor DeWitt?" He reached for his iPad to take notes.

"We're colleagues at the GSD. That's Harvard's architecture school."

"Yes, I know." He smiled charmingly, but Iris was feeling immune to charm these last few days. Still, she couldn't help noting the dimple on his left cheek. "I'm a practicing architect as well as a teacher. Xander had told me about a new type of self-cleaning glass that I'd like to use on a project I'm designing in Harvard Square. I couldn't remember the name of the manufacturer, and Xander wasn't answering his cell phone. I was going out anyway to walk my dog, so I thought I'd drop a note through his mail slot."

"Which day are we talking about?"

"Wednesday, the night Lara disappeared."

Martin Taylor stopped typing. "Did you see him?"

"Yes, I saw him through the living room window, but he didn't see me." Iris could feel her cheeks heating up.

"Did you ring the doorbell? What time was this?"

"Around nine. I didn't want to bother Xander because I

noticed he was in his pajamas, listening to music, I assume. He had a big set of headphones on. I told Xander about this a few days afterward and he said he would tell his lawyer about this alibi. Well, partial alibi. Since that time the police have learned that Lara was actually abducted at around ten, so Xander still might have gone out after I saw him at home."

Martin's fingers fluttered over his keyboard, then stopped abruptly. He rubbed his chin but didn't say anything.

Despite his pause, Iris continued. "But I've been thinking about it. According to her father's account in the newspaper, Lara always stayed at home at night, after her father went out. That night though, she went to a friend's house at around nine. "

Martin looked at her sharply. "How do you know?"

"Because I know the friend. I think the kidnapper must have been stalking Lara. He must have followed her to Ja—, the friend's apartment, then taken the opportunity to grab Lara when her friend went out."

"And Xander couldn't have been stalking Lara at nine since you saw him at that time in his living room."

"Exactly!"

"And Lara's friend, she can testify as well?"

"No, she doesn't want to be involved. The police have her

testimony but they've agreed to keep her out of this."

Martin pressed his lips together.

"Xander told me that he thinks someone's framing him and planting evidence in his house," Iris said. "I think it may be his assistant, Nils Jensen."

"Do you know of any motive this Mr. Jensen would have to want to get Professor DeWitt in trouble?"

"Well— I think he might have a crush on Xander, and if his feelings weren't reciprocated... He also has easy access to Xander's house."

"That's certainly worth looking into." Martin sank back into his chair. "Don't take this the wrong way, but I have to ask you. You and the professor—it sounds like you're close. Is it a romantic relationship?"

"No, no. We're just colleagues. I want to set the record straight so we can all learn the truth about what happened that night."

Martin gave her a brief look of incredulity, then shuttered it. "Admirable." He looked down at his notes. "Anything else you can think of?"

"No. Just that the kidnapper must have been stalking Lara that night around the time I saw Xander."

Martin's eyes were serious. "This is critical information, Iris. Jim will want to speak with you as soon as I fill him in about this. It's possible that Professor DeWitt has already mentioned this to Jim, but it makes a difference that you've volunteered to act as the professor's alibi."

Iris started to unconsciously shred her thumb nail.

"I wish that all witnesses had your desire for justice." He slipped a business card out of his vest pocket, then flipped it over to scribble something. "I'm giving you my cell phone number. Call me if you think of anything else. In any case, we'll be in touch soon."

Iris felt buzzed with importance when she left the conference room. But a few minutes later, as the elevator descended from the thirtieth floor, the full import hit her: far from distancing herself from this case, she had now volunteered to become the star witness for the defense. Why couldn't she control her compulsive need to ferret out the truth? Why couldn't she just back the hell away from trouble?

CHAPTER 54

It was ten the next morning by the time Xander had been bailed out of that wretched place and Farrington had dropped him off at the Howland Street house. The solicitor assured him that he'd be in touch soon to plan their strategy. All Xander wanted was a hot shower.

He crossed to the kitchen as he fumbled for his pack of Gauloise. His jailers had brought watery scrambled eggs, toast, and disgusting coffee to his cell at the ungodly hour of six. Not that he had been sleeping.

Maybe the shower could wait. He needed a cup of decent coffee first. He filled his espresso pot and, while it was heating up, his cell phone buzzed.

Caller I.D. displayed the name of one of the partners in his Amsterdam office. Xander sank into a chair before punching the button. "Stefan, I'm surprised to hear from you. Is everything all right?"

"No, Xander, it isn't. We've had a call from our New York client asking about a news story he just saw on the internet. It says you've been arrested for murder—the murder of a young girl." Stefan spat out the word 'murder.' "Joos and I are waiting to hear your explanation before we decide on what action to take. Are these allegations true?"

"No, of course not. I've done nothing wrong, Stefan. I've never even met this girl. My solicitor got me out on bail and he'll straighten this out. I should sue that news outlet for libel. I can't believe they'd put such a thing on the internet!"

Xander scurried to his study and booted up his laptop. "What website is this story on?"

"It's on the *New York Post*'s Page Six section. Were you actually arrested?"

"Technically, but it's a false arrest. You've heard about how the American police harass foreigners."

"What is this business about child pornography being found on your computer? It cites an unnamed source inside the police department. That's not something someone states without proof. We design schools, for God's sake!"

The *New York Post*'s page came up and its top story made Xander's heart jump into his throat: *Harvard Professor Charged in*

Girl's Disappearance. A sob issued from him.

"I'm sorry, Xander, but Joos and I will be meeting tomorrow morning at nine with our marketing and P.R. people to decide how to handle the fallout from this. Dieter's Skyping us from Beijing for the meeting so we can take a vote. For the time being we need to distance ourselves from you until you can straighten this out. I suggest you get your solicitor to try to contain this scandal."

"But it's my firm. You can't meet without me."

"We have a morals clause in our partnership agreement. In fact, you're the one who put it in."

"How dare you imply that I'm immoral!"

"I'm not the one saying it. The *New York Post* is. And, by the end of the day, everyone will be repeating it."

"We've been partners for five years, Stefan. You need to give me some time before you take any votes or issue any statements."

"I'm afraid we can't. You've put our firm in jeopardy. We have to do something to hang onto our clients." There was a pause, then, "Good luck," before the line went dead.

Xander returned frantically to the *Post* article. *A well-known 40-year-old Dutch architect, a visiting professor at Harvard's Graduate School of Design, has been charged with the kidnapping and murder of Lara Kurjak, the twelve-year-old girl whose disappearance has riveted the Boston area for the last week. An unnamed source at the Cambridge Police Department says that child pornography was found on the professor's computer.*

So the police *had* discovered those pictures on his computer. Nils hadn't been able to scrub them completely from the damn hard drive after all. The *Post* hadn't actually disclosed his name, but it would take even the laziest reporter nothing but a quick trip to the GSD website to track that down.

Xander scurried to the living room window and peered out from between the curtains. No reporters were camped out on the sidewalk yet but he spotted a gray Prius across the street with what looked like two shadows inside—no doubt undercover police. He speed-dialed Checker Cab on his way upstairs and told them to have someone wait around the corner on Hammond Street. After tossing some clothes, a toiletry bag, and his passport into a leather duffle bag, Xander slipped out the kitchen door and wedged himself through a gap in the backyard fence where the corner posts didn't quite meet. He jogged toward the yellow cab and freedom.

Once the cab had pulled away from the curb, he punched in the KLM phone number to make a reservation. He would figure out how to solve this crisis after he was comfortably ensconced in his favorite business class seat, sipping a double single-malt

Scotch. He smoothed the vents of his Brunello Cucinelli jacket under him to keep them from wrinkling. This is what he excelled at—solving crises. Hadn't he convinced the Dubai Museum Committee to open the spigot wider after the construction budget ballooned to twice his original promise? Hadn't he ressurrected his firm's bid for the Vienna Convention Center after his partners had given up hope, leading them to winning the commission?

Maybe he wouldn't go back to the States after this. He'd stay in Europe, like Roman Polanski. The priggish Americans could gnash their teeth. Nils could finish teaching the damn Harvard course.

That's what Nietsche would do.

CHAPTER 55

Budge caught a flash of yellow in the corner of his eye and twisted in his seat, suddenly on full alert. He spotted Xander squeezing through an opening in his back yard fence, then heading toward an idling Checker Cab, and thanked the journalistic gods for inspiring him to park at this perfect vantage point.

"Shane—showtime. Wake up. Quarry's at four o'clock!"

"Whah?" The gangly photographer yawned, untangling his limbs in the passenger seat as Budge maneuvered the tiny Fiat half-way out of its parking space.

What Budge saw next in the rearview mirror made him cut the engine and leap out of the car. He raced toward Iris, finger over his lips.

Iris waved him away. "I don't have time now, Budge. I have to catch Xander. I see him up ahead getting into a cab."

"No, you can't warn him. Here, get in my car. We can discuss this while I follow him." He shoved Iris into the back seat, hit the child lock, and slid back behind the wheel. As he eased out onto Hammond Street, he could see the taxi pulling away from the curb.

"You can't kidnap me," she screamed while straightening herself into a sitting position. "I need to speak to Xander." She rummaged in her purse for her phone.

"Shane, show her the *Post* article."

Shane brought it up on his phone and passed it back to her.

"How am I supposed to read this in a moving car?" Iris groused as she enlarged the print. She scanned the paragraph. "Child pornography?" She looked momentarily stunned, then, remembering Xander's explanation, said, "This must have been planted by the person setting him up."

"Then why's he running? He's been arrested, just got out on bail, the *Post* outs him as a predator, and his reaction is to call a cab and sneak out his backyard with an overnight bag?"

"He's probably scared because you vultures are hounding him," Iris said. "Maybe he's going to check into a hotel for some privacy."

"He's making a run for it, mark my words," Budge said. "You are about to witness Cambridge's version of O.J. Simpson in the white Ford Bronco."

"Except you're not the police." Iris crossed her arms. "If

you're right, what do you intend to do—make a citizen's arrest? You just want to grab headlines at his expense."

"Yeah, what did happen to those cops in the Prius?" Shane asked as he whipped open his video camera case and snapped on a long lens.

"They only had eyes on the front door. You snooze, you lose in this business."

"We really should call them, Buchanan." Shane flipped off his lens cap.

"We will, we will. Let's see if the cab turns left at the Wine Cask and heads toward Union Square. That's a straight line toward Logan. Meanwhile, get a shot of the back of the cab. Can you zoom in on his head?"

"Yup. I'm zooming in but the dude's facing forward." Shane lowered his window and started to lift the camera.

"No!" Budge shouted. "Keep it inside. Don't let him see the camera. You'll spook him," After the cab turned left onto Washington Street, Budge tapped in a number on the car visor's phone pad.

Detective Malone identified himself on the speakerphone and Budge filled him in.

"Where are my guys? Never mind. I'll find out myself. Can you tell whether DeWitt is armed?"

"I don't think so." Budge's knuckles turned white as he gripped the steering wheel.

"In that case, are you comfortable continuing to follow the taxi?"

"Hell, yes!" Shane called out.

"Stay on the line then so you can keep feeding my partner the cab's position. We're heading out to join you."

Budge stayed one or two cars behind as pursued and pursuer proceeded along McGrath Highway, through interminable lights, and over the Museum of Science bridge. Budge noticed a Honda Accord with two passengers sidle in next to the cab. He borrowed Shane's phone to alert his editor to leave space on the front page for his scoop.

At one point, Budge shouted to Iris over his shoulder, "Stop clutching the front seat.! You're worse than a toddler on a plane."

"Stop complaining. You're the one who kidnapped me," she snapped back at him. Why did this man always reduce her to his level of playground taunts?

The cab crossed into Boston and dropped down into the

Central Artery tunnel, hugging the right lane. Shane rested the camera on the dash and let it record. "Looks like he's taking the Callahan tunnel. Definitely heading to Logan."

The cabbie emerged from the tunnel and veered onto the airport exit ramp, blind to the two cars tailing him. They all followed the ring road, then turned off at Terminal E for international departures at the far side of the airport. Budge quickly weighed the option of abandoning his car at the terminal to face certain towing against the chance of missing any soundbites uttered at the fleeing Dutchman's re-arrest.

"Iris, you stay in the car. Circle around if you have to."

"Fat chance. I'm coming in too," she said.

Budge bared his teeth at her.

"Just try to stop me," she dared him.

In the end, they all piled out. No question that Shane needed to be there to record the panicked look on DeWitt's face for that killer front page visual.

"Keep the camera hidden, Shane. Iris, we hang back since he knows us. The cops won't thank us if we tip him off."

Five sets of eyes watched Xander pay his cab fare and saunter into the terminal. After a pained parting look at the Fiat,

Budge, followed by Iris and Shane, trailed Xander at a cautious distance. Shane kept his jacket slung over his arm carrying the video camera.

One of Logan's famously cranky state troopers ran toward the Fiat, arms waving.

CHAPTER 56

Budge followed in Xander's wake, trailed closely by Iris and Shane. Xander was quickly swallowed up inside the cavernous terminal. After scanning the crowd at Aer Lingus and Iberia, Iris picked out Xander's elegant camel hair jacket veering toward the KLM business class check-in line. She gave Budge a poke in the ribs, and pointed. He gestured for them to follow him into the KLM economy line that snaked through several endless loops.

Budge whipped a Red Sox cap out of his pocket and jammed it low over his eyes. Shane hid his camera under his anorak, but kept his eyes trained on Xander. Iris rummaged in her purse and retrieved a crumpled rain hat and a pair of sunglasses.

An elderly man in a wheelchair and his attendant waited for their luggage to be weighed. They watched the business class agent typing on her computer. Next in line, Xander fished his passport out of a jacket pocket.

Iris spotted Malone hiding behind a building column. She looked around until she saw Russo, hiding behind the arrivals display board. He caught her eye and signaled "scram" with his thumb. She ignored him.

"I can't believe this guy is stupid enough to try to bolt," Shane murmured.

"Malone and Russo are watching," Iris said.

"I hope they've called the Staties for back-up," Budge said. "The Cambridge police don't have jurisdiction on airport property."

"You mean those guys in jodphers out ticketing cars—they're the ones who need to arrest Xander?" Iris asked.

Budge grimaced at the mention of cars being ticketed. "Except when the locals chase a perp who never leaves their sight and ends up here at Logan. That's called 'the chain of fresh pursuit'. The cops lost eyes on DeWitt when he left his house, remember? I'm the one who called Malone to alert him to DeWitt's running."

Iris was impressed.

"I know this stuff because I'm a crime reporter, and a damn good one," Budge finished modestly.

Iris glanced back over to Malone who was having an animated discussion with his lapel. She hoped for his sake there was a hidden phone in his pocket.

"Doesn't the Judge usually take away your passport when you're out on bail?" Iris asked.

"Kinda makes you think the D.A. might've been hoping DeWitt would try something like this." Budge said. "Fleeing definitely makes him look guilty."

Xander stepped up to the agent and flashed a charming smile as he lifted his small duffle to show her his hand luggage. The agent's attention quickly reverted to her computer.

Budge nudged Shane.

Shane aimed his anorak at Xander.

Malone's eyes grew round at Xander's progress and Shane's recording of it. He was too far away to hear, but Iris could see his lips moving briskly.

The agent slid Xander's boarding pass and passport across the counter. He shifted the duffle back onto his shoulder.

When Xander turned to peer at the overhead display, Iris ducked her head and Budge pulled his cap lower on his forehead.

Xander sauntered toward the security lines.

Malone followed at a discrete distance. Russo sprinted toward the oversized exit doors.

Budge and Shane were as alert as bird dogs and seemed to be communicating telepathically. All three of them turned as one toward the security checkpoint.

Xander slipped through business class security, then the scanner.

Malone palmed his badge and flashed the TSA agent in the line for airline pilots and staff. They waved him through.

Iris, Budge, and Shane approached pre-screening.

"I don't care if you're press. You don't have a boarding pass. Get out of the line," the agent said.

They trudged off to one side and leaned against a wall, dejected.

"Doesn't look like we're going to get close to the action," Shane said.

"They have to come out this way after they arrest DeWitt and I need that money shot of him in cuffs for the front page."

"Unless I end up taking a shot of his plane taking off with him on it instead. I don't see any staties around," Shane said.

Iris heard footsteps running toward her. She turned and saw Russo and an overweight state trooper, red-faced and panting.

Russo and the Statie flashed badges and Russo whispered something to the TSA agent. The security line was closed off and the line began to back up. Irritated passengers looked at their watches and phones.

"My plane's taking off in ten minutes," a man in a trench coat complained loudly.

"What's going on? Is it a terrorist threat?" a worried-looking woman asked her husband.

Iris stood on tiptoes, but the walkway split sideways after security so she couldn't see very far.

What is Xander doing, Iris wondered. Why is he running away? I was going to give him an alibi. He must be guilty. Clearly he planned to fly off to someplace without extradition and escape punishment for what he'd done to poor Lara. They would never find out the truth behind what had happened and why.

Then Iris saw Xander racing down the corridor in her direction, shouldering his way through milling passengers, heading for the escalator. She saw Russo weaving through the same obstacle course of suitcase-rolling passengers, but he was too far behind. Xander was going to get away!

Shane lifted his camera onto his shoulder, all pretense of secrecy gone.

That's when something in Iris snapped.

She shoved over the roped stanchions and raced through the body scanner. She passed the rolling baggage belt, and the startled TSA agents. At a full run, Iris slid into a leg sweep, hooking

Xander's ankle and bringing him down. He toppled in a heap on top of her, cursing loudly in, presumably, Dutch. As her arm bent at a distorted angle, Iris let out an agonized cry.

Russo closed the gap between them, yanked Xander to his feet, grabbed his hands behind him, and slipped on cuffs. Close behind him, Malone rushed up and helped Iris to her feet by her uninjured arm.

"Where did you come from? Malone asked her. "That was amazing."

CHAPTER 57

Iris was strapped into the passenger seat of Sterling's Lexus, gingerly adjusting her new plaster cast above the seatbelt, tuning out Sterling's scolding. She still couldn't believe that she'd blocked Xander's escape using a karate takedown. She was probably in for another lecture from Sensei Ono about Uechiryu being a self-defense-oriented martial art, not to be used for aggressive purposes. She also knew she'd have to endure ridicule from her fellow karate students. At the speed she'd been moving, her leg sweep, caught no doubt by Shane's camera, would have looked like some macho Bruce Lee flying side-kick. This was the opposite of the type of subtle, close-in fighting her school of karate taught. The dramatic move had cost her a broken arm, but at least it was her left arm, not her drafting arm.

Sterling had finished his lecture and was now concentrating on dodging cyclists as he drove through the back streets of Cambridge. The pain of the fractured radius bone in her arm had been dulled by the meds supplied by the doctor at Mass General's emergency room. Luckily, she hadn't needed surgery, only some realignment and a cast to hold her arm in place.

While she was being tended to in the emergency room at Mass General, Sterling had placated the cranky people at TSA and the state police for her transgressions on their turf. Given the satisfactory outcome achieved at her own personal risk, they were willing to drop the charges for her breaking through their security line without a boarding pass.

"You realize, of course, that this whole debacle will be on the six o'clock news, thanks to your buddy with the video camera," Sterling said, pulling into her driveway.

"Not my buddy," Iris said. "Thanks for the rescue, Sterling."

Iris managed to unlock her front door with one hand, and to sort through the mess of mail in her entry hall. She sacrificed a junk mail envelope into Sheba's waiting mouth, to be dumped on the kitchen floor in exchange for a treat—one of the least useful tricks Iris had ever taught the dog.

The clock on her microwave read four o'clock and she realized that she hadn't eaten since breakfast. She opened the refrigerator door, surveyed its contents, then closed it again. She wasn't hungry.

She fished out Martin Taylor's business card and her phone from her purse. After composing an excuse for her change of heart into words that she hoped sounded convincing, she dialed the lawyer's office number. Of course he wasn't available, so she left her message on his voice mail.

Iris was too restless to do any work in her office in the next room, and she'd already called Ellie from the hospital, so she headed instead to the basement. She needed to demolish something.

Her ongoing plan to build a sculpture studio required her to reconfigure the existing two underground rooms. The utility and storage rooms would be made smaller, creating space for a third room large enough to fit a band saw, a planer and a joiner for assembling huge wood blocks. These she would carve into abstract, organic shapes. Having a self-contained studio would keep the wood shavings and mess generated from infiltrating the entire basement.

She stuffed some rags into the crack under the door at the top of the stairs to keep plaster dust from filtering up into the house, then changed into a tee-shirt and ripped jeans. Only one of the three walls she needed to remove was structural. She would need help in erecting a beam to hold up the weight of the floor above it, but that left two walls that she could safely attack today. She lifted a crow bar down from its hook on the wall. There were no plumbing pipes in this first wall, but there were sure to be electric wires, so she'd have to proceed carefully. Once she'd chipped off the horsehair plaster and peeled back the lath, she could whale on the vertical studs with her crow bar to work herself into a satisfying state of exhaustion.

By the time one wall was completely down, Iris was covered in a fine layer of gray dust. Her broken arm was sore and sweaty in its cast, but she didn't care. Waiting for the air to clear, she heard Sheba's long, drawn out baying overhead. As she mounted the stairs, she could hear the doorbell ringing.

Iris slid the dust mask onto the top of her head. Her hair, already gray-tinged with plaster, now stuck out in tufts. She opened her front door to reveal Martin Taylor, immaculate in a navy pin-striped suit, on the front porch. He looked momentarily surprised.

"I heard about your ordeal at the airport and thought maybe you could use this." He held up a bottle of wine. "How's your arm?"

"Not too bad, thanks, but I probably shouldn't be doing one-armed demolition in the basement."

Martin cocked an eyebrow. "You know, you can pay people to do that."

This remark irked Iris, but she stood aside to let him enter. Sheba growled quietly and stayed close to her mistress.

"Sorry for dropping by unannounced but you're on my route home and I was hoping to discuss the message you left," he said, taking in her large hallway and casting Sheba an appraising look.

Iris led him to the living room. She glanced down at her dusty jeans, then decided to remain standing. Martin did the same.

"Today's been discouraging for all of us with DeWitt trying to jump bail, but he probably just panicked after a night in jail." Martin looked at her earnestly. "That doesn't change what you saw that night. It will be up to a jury to put the pieces together to figure out if he's guilty or not, but that requires giving them all the pieces. Otherwise the system doesn't work."

Iris leaned against the door frame. "I'm not comfortable anymore being part of his defense and, since I'm the one who stopped him from getting away today, I'm sure he doesn't want me on his team."

"I understand. DeWitt did a wrong thing today. He was scared and confused. If you'd feel more comfortable, we can call you as a hostile witness. Just tell the jury what you saw and when. I know you want to get to the truth like the rest of us."

Iris closed her eyes and sighed.

"What do you say we have a glass of wine?" Martin said. "You've had a rough day,"

"That's an excellent idea." She led him to the kitchen and got out a corkscrew and two wine glasses, checking them first for water spots.

The doorbell rang again and Sheba scurried toward it. Who else would be dropping by now?

When she opened the door, Luc was standing there looking frazzled. He wore a black apron over his jeans and held a paper bag which gave off an amazing aroma. Iris felt like hugging him.

"I saw the thing on TV. Are you alright?" He reached out and patted her cast, looked at her shyly, then crouched down to scratch Sheba behind the ears. The dog leaned against him.

"Hell of a day." Iris said. "How're you doing?"

Luc rose to his feet, and began to say something. Then his eyes turned flat.

Iris turned and saw Martin standing behind her in the doorway holding two glasses of wine.

Luc handed her the bag. "I just wanted to drop this off. I left Eduardo in charge of the kitchen. I hope the arm's better soon." Then he left.

As Iris watched Luc's retreating form, Martin handed her a glass and said, "What's in the bag?"

CHAPTER 58

"**G**irl, you're turning schizo," Ellie said on Monday morning as Iris walked into their shared office with her laptop propped under her cast.

"First, you tackle an escaping suspect, now you're back on the team to exonerate him. Whose side are you on?"

Iris shook her head. "I just need to find out the truth. I can't stop thinking about the girl. We'd never have learned what happened to her if Xander had run away. We still might not find out after a trial. But Martin pointed out— "

"Martin—that's the lawyer? You're on a first-name basis now? What's going on with Luc?"

"Don't even ask," Iris said as she rummaged in her desk drawer for a Kit-Kat bar, unwrapped it, and bit off a piece. "Did you arrange things with the computer wizard, Elvis?"

"I did, and I'd better not get any blowback. I spent most of last semester trying to discourage his crush. I mention my dear husband and college-aged daughter every chance I can, but nothing seems to dampen his ardor. He said he'd meet you at the Starbucks by the Broadway Market at nine."

Iris consulted her watch as she shoved the rest of the candy bar into her mouth.

"Elvis said he saw your takedown of Professor DeWitt on YouTube. He sounded impressed."

"It's on YouTube? Swell. I thought I was getting some weird looks as I passed through the studio just now," Iris said. "Gilles is probably going to fire me."

"Your hero act has either canceled out his mistake in hiring a murderer or it's given GSD a reputation for having cuckoo professors."

"How did I ever get mixed up with Xander DeWitt?" Iris threw her purse over a shoulder. "Gotta go meet Elvis. I'll tell him you say hi."

Iris spent the four block walk to Starbucks reviewing what she wanted to learn from the computer wizard. As she awkwardly pushed through the front door with her cast arm, she spotted a young Asian man in shorts and flip-flops sitting at a table reading the *Globe*. When he saw her he held up the front page—Shane's shot of her midair body block of the oncoming Xander. She had to admit she looked pretty kick-ass.

"Way to go, Professor Reid," he shouted.

She fluttered her good hand in a keep-it-down gesture and looked around self-consciously. No one in the shop paid her any attention. She slid into the seat across from him and shrugged out of her jacket. "Thanks for meeting with me, Elvis. I'm hoping you can help me with some computer questions."

"No problem. What do you want to know?"

"First, I need you to keep what we discuss completely confidential. You can't talk about this with anyone. Are you comfortable with that?"

"But Ellie, I mean Professor McKensie, is in on this, isn't she?"

"You can't even discuss this with Professor McKensie, OK?" The last thing Ellie would want would be Elvis imagining some shared secret.

Elvis slid his chair closer and lowered his voice to be just audible above the hissing and sputtering of the coffee machines. "My lips are sealed."

"I understand you helped Professor McKensie retrieve some information on her computer last semester, files she thought she had erased accidently."

"Yeah, her computer crashed and, if you can believe it, she hadn't backed up some files, so I trawled through her hard drive and used some recovery software to pull out fragments and recreate the files. Basic stuff."

"And... if you wanted to put something incriminating on my computer without getting caught, how would you go about it ?"

Elvis raised his eyes to the acoustical tile ceiling. "I would probably send you an e-mail from an internet café or a library using a free e-mail address. If I wanted to get fancy, I could use a web anonymizer or web onion to ping off satellites around the world to mask where I was sending it from. Then I'd include a logic bomb so it would self-destruct after you read it." His eyes glistened. "I wouldn't want anything sent from my own computer because even if I cyber-scrubbed the hard drive, the forensic techs could still recover ghosts. Then again, *you* wouldn't be able to completely erase the stuff I sent either."

"How about if you had direct access to my computer? Let's say you broke into my house and knew my password."

"That's easy. I'd just download some evil stuff—like how to make a bomb or something. The FBI is often tracking who goes to those kinds of sites. If you noticed it later on your browsing history, you could try to erase it but, like I said, that stuff leaves ghosts that techies can dig out."

Iris chewed on this information. "That's just what I needed

to know. Thanks." She wanted to shift gears without having Elvis notice the transition. "I need a latte. Can I get you something?"

After she returned with their drinks she started up again, "I know you're in Professor DeWitt's seminar this semester. Who's going to teach the class now that he's in jail?"

"Gilles said that the professor's assistant Nils was going to take over until someone from their Amsterdam office could fly over."

"I don't really think of Nils as a teacher. I thought he was more of a tech guy."

"He's an all-purpose TA. I'm really bummed because I wanted to study with someone of Professor DeWitt's caliber."

"I'm sure Xander's firm will send someone high-powered."

"I guess." Elvis finished off his coffee.

"One more thing," Iris said. "Earlier this semester I was having trouble getting onto my GSD network account. My password no longer worked. I eventually changed to a new password, but now I'm thinking that someone might have hacked into my account. Does that sound likely or am I just being paranoid?"

"In this day and age, there's no such thing as paranoid. Your worst fears are reality. If you want to leave it with me now, I can run some software to detect if any spyware was planted on it. I can run the program while I'm in the studio, then drop off your laptop at your GSD office. It will take me about half an hour."

"Seriously? That would be great. I'd really appreciate it."

At that moment the reality of knowing whether someone had been reading her e-mails hit Iris, making her skin prickle. "If you find anything, you can take it off—right?"

"Of course." Elvis looked affronted. "You know, putting spyware on someone's computer is pretty heavy stuff—illegal even. It would take someone with pretty high-caliber computer chops to pull that off."

"Do you know of anyone at GSD with those kinds of skills?"

He paused in thought. "I couldn't say for sure but rumor has it that there's someone in your studio who's quite the cyber-freak. They say she broke into the GSD main servers last year and the administration never even noticed. She's that good."

"Who are we talking about?"

He started shredding his wooden stir stick into little pieces. "I don't know if I should say. You're not going to get her in trouble, are you?"

"No, not at all."

Elvis leaned over conspiratorially, "It's Jasna. Jasna Sidron."

CHAPTER 59

Xander always expected to be famous, just not for this. Not for killing a young girl.

The morning after his ignominious capture at Logan, he sat across from his two solicitors in a tiny airless interview room in the bowels of the Cambridge police station, staring at himself on the front page of the *Globe*.

Farrington tapped the newspaper. "I'm not going to sugarcoat this, Xander. Your attempt to jump bail yesterday has given the D.A. the upper hand. You're being transferred later today to Walpole, a maximum security prison.

"How long will I have to be there?" Xander asked, his lips tightening.

Farrington paged through some papers in front of him, found the one he was looking for, consulted it, then announced, "Your trial's been set for mid-March, six months from now. You'll be held at Walpole until then."

Xander felt nothing but shock.

Farrington went on. "You need to understand: yesterday, we had a no body, no weapon, sketchy-motive case. The burden was on the state to string together enough circumstantial evidence to convince a jury beyond a reasonable doubt. But now, the pendulum has swung. The Cambridge police's Cyber Forensics lab has found child pornography on your computer. Someone attempted to erase the images, but they've reformatted your hard drive and found it. If you're a pedophile, you could have a motive for kidnapping and possibly murdering the girl. Furthermore, your attempt to flee yesterday makes you appear guilty."

Xander rubbed his temples and stared at the metal table between them. "Those images were planted when my house was broken into. I called my assistant, Nils, to make sure they were taken off my computer immediately. What was I supposed to do?"

He could see Farrington and the well-dressed younger lawyer exchange quick looks. The younger man asked, "Did you think about reporting those pictures to the police?"

"No, I assumed they were spam or some sick joke. I had told the police the night before that nothing appeared to be missing after the break-in."

Farrington cleared his throat and held up a hand, ticking off points with his fingers one by one. "In addition to the preteen porn on your computer, the police found a witness who directed the girl to your office days before she disappeared. The keys to the kidnapper's van were found in your kitchen drawer, despite your story about having no access to a vehicle. Lara's necklace was in that same van. They have Lara's blood—enough to strongly suggest her death—on a bedspread found in a barn near a place you visited the week before, a barn where an imprint of your boot was found that, with Lara's blood on one sole, was retrieved from your house. Then there's the business of your trying to leave the country while out on bail. A skilled prosecutor can weave these pieces together to construct a convincing case." He stopped and looked at his companion. "Martin, have I forgotten anything?"

"The crossing of state lines," Martin said. "The fact that Lara's blood was found in New Hampshire suggests that she may have been killed there, which would make this a federal crime instead of a Massachusetts crime."

"What is the significance of that?" Xander asked, feeling a cold dread in the pit of his stomach.

Martin broke eye contact. "Massachusetts doesn't have the death penalty, but the D.A. can request it for a federal crime."

289

Xander felt the room go blurry. He tried to grip the edge of the cold metal table to steady himself but sensed himself slipping off his chair before everything went dark.

CHAPTER 60

His new cell at MCI-Cedar Junction in Walpole, an hour south of Boston, made the holding cell in Cambridge look like the Ritz. The main structure was a Brutalist concrete bunker—the 1960's were a disastrous time for prison architecture—surrounded by twenty foot high walls with guard towers. They had strip-searched him before giving him itchy gray scrubs to wear and canvas shoes that kept slipping off his elegant narrow feet.

His first meal, lunch, had filled him with horror at what lay ahead. He couldn't even identify the meat in the sandwiches, much less the other offerings. In any case, he felt too nauseated to eat. Maybe he should go on a hunger strike. Would that get him out of this place any sooner?

In Cambridge he had had a cell to himself. Here, he had a large, disreputable-looking roommate called The Ram who was presently out in the trampled dirt area they called "the yard," lifting weights or doing something equally macho. He would have to figure out a way to handle The Ram, to convince the lug to act as his protector in this place.

Xander tried not to blame himself for the fiasco the day before. He might have escaped if that crazy Iris Reid hadn't barreled into him like an S-class Mercedes hitting a smart car on the Autobahn.

Plus, his idiot solicitors didn't seem to believe him. He would have to use his own superior intellect and charisma to spring himself from this Kafkaesque nightmare. Didn't prisons have libraries? He'd brush up on the law and use some clever argument to win his case. Then maybe he'd write a book about his ordeal.

No question that someone was framing him, but why? He might have stepped on toes in his climb toward the top of his profession. Someone might have resented his meteoric rise. Or maybe it was because he was, well, different.

If only he could have felt genuine lust at the sight of a grown woman's breast, maybe none of this would have happened. It had taken him many years to understand what he really needed. Reading Nietszche's *Man and Superman* as a teenager had reassured him that he was special, somehow above the others, an outlier. When he developed a fascination for a friend's younger sister, it became clear that he was drawn to the purity of innocence.

For some reason that girl hadn't responded to his overtures, but he knew there would be other chances with other girls.

In college, he had focused on his studies. There had been no one there he could really talk to. They were all like children, and hadn't developed yet. He rose to the top of his class, even giving a rousing graduation speech featuring expansive references to, of course, Nietszche.

He followed his inspiration's path by entering military service next and liked the regimentation involved. He chose to join the UN peacekeeping forces and was sent to Bosnia, utterly unprepared for the savagery he witnessed there: Serbs and Croats butchering each other, then both turning on the Muslim Bosnians. It was a place without morals. The peacekeepers were in constant danger from snipers who would as soon pick them off as kill their sworn enemies.

Then one day, his battalion unearthed one of the Serb's dumping pits. The Serbs had tried to disguise the stench by piling dog carcasses on top of the dead bodies of Bosnian males from ten to sixty, two dozen of them. On their way back to camp, Xander's batallion passed through a village and ran into an ambush. A sniper wounded his teammate, Nils, before Xander could drag him to safety. They put Nils on a medical truck, leaving Xander to patrol alone for the rest of that week.

What followed next seemed like fate. He spotted a girl racing through the woods like a fawn. She was filthy, but still fresh with the innocence of youth. If she had stayed in the woods for long, the barbarian Serbs would have found her and defiled her. Xander couldn't let that happen. He had to show her some beauty amidst the ugliness of war.

He plucked her up in his arms and found a rustic shed nearby. Here, he initiated her into the mysteries of sex. It had been a mystery for him too, but he had played his role well. Ungrateful, she had bit him hard on his hand. He still had an ugly scar. Still, the girl's bite had electrified him.

He had kept her in the shed for several days, smuggling her food from the canteen. But it soon occurred to him that what he had done might be misconstrued. His attempt to lift himself and this wild child above the war zone might be labeled, by less sensitive souls, as something base, even criminal, if it were ever discovered. Also, the girl did not seem to appreciate the risks he was taking for her. He had needed to devise a way to get rid of her without having blood on his hands.

Ever since that first time, he had tried to duplicate the adrenaline high he had experienced while being surrounded by so much danger. But even in Thailand, with willing participants, he had yet to recreate that spark.

CHAPTER 61

On exiting Starbucks, Iris mindlessly followed Broadway past the Fogg Museum, still shrouded under scaffolding, and drifted across Quincy Street to enter Harvard Yard. She needed to think. She eyed the imposing steps of Widener Library, then turned toward Memorial Church across an expansive green.

She entered the sanctuary through the main porch and slipped into a velvet-cushioned pew. The elegant, barrel-vaulted space was empty.

Iris bowed her head, closed her eyes, and thought about what it would take to kill someone. The typical reasons—jealousy, anger, and greed—wouldn't apply if the victim was a young girl, especially the type of utterly blameless girl that Lara appeared to have been. Maybe she could find out more about the girl from Jasna. Iris couldn't imagine the intensity of twisted hatred needed to stab, or shoot, or strangle the angelic Lara. So the motive must have been lust. Power or lust.

Iris couldn't stand the thought of the perpetrator getting away with murder. But she still couldn't believe that the man with whom she had briefly shared her innermost thoughts was behind Lara's death. Perhaps she had no real sense of the man. It would have taken powerful emotions, passion and hatred, to do something so vicious. And her impression of Xander was that all of his passion went into his career.

Maybe Martin was right that Xander's attempt to escape had come from panic at the possibility of being falsely accused and convicted, not a knowledge of actual guilt.

Martin—she had barely been able to slug down her glass of wine before thinking of an excuse to get him to leave. Why had she invited the lawyer in? Watching Luc walk away had left her emotionally gutted.

Before her time with Luc, Iris had been used to being on her own. She needed her independence and liked her life clean. But the months she had spent with him had shifted that equilibrium. It hadn't hurt that he was incredible in bed. But then she had run into his lie, an important part of his life that he had kept from her. Why hadn't she sensed that he was holding something back? How could she trust her judgment about anyone anymore?

CHAPTER 62

Iris plodded back to her GSD office to see what Elvis had discovered. She found a note stuck to her laptop. It said: "Professor Reid, there was some serious spyware on here, routed through several dummy sites, but I tracked it down to Jasna Sidron's computer. I took it off your hard drive so you're safe now. E."

Iris pulled on a sweater from her desk drawer to ward off a sudden chill and sank into her desk chair. She stared out the window at the High Victorian spire of Memorial Hall. Jasna had intercepted all of her e-mails, sent and received. Why? What had she discussed in them? She'd have to reread them all.

Forty minutes before, while sitting in the church pew, Iris had decided that she needed to question Jasna more about Lara's life. Now she had a second reason to track down her student. She needed to discover why Jasna was spying on her.

Iris settled her shoulders then descended the stairs to see if

Jasna was working at her desk. As expected, on a day when design studio didn't meet, Jasna's pod was empty, so Iris trudged to her Jeep and headed over to Bay State Road where her student lived in one of the few West Cambridge neighborhoods not yet gentrified.

Finding no empty visitor parking space, she backtracked to park on a side street in a Cambridge residents spot and walked back to the apartment building. She leaned on Jasna's buzzer and waited. As she watched, a curtain flickered in Jasna's second floor window but there was no response to the intercom.

Iris was trying to decide on her next step, when the front door groaned open and a familiar-looking terrier leapt joyfully out at Iris, straining on its leash. Mr. Demopoulos eyed her through his thick lenses, yanking Sparky back, until recognition dawned. "You're that teacher Jasna brought by," he announced.

"That's right. I'm here to see her. Let me hold the door for you."

The old man, wearing a worn chenille bathrobe which exposed his white chest hair, shuffled out at the end of Sparky's leash, allowing Iris to slip in behind him. She climbed to the second floor and knocked on the front door of Jasna's apartment.

As on Iris' previous visit, she could hear Jasna speaking, in French, through the flimsy hollowcore door. "*Il me faut dire au revoir au moment, Cherie.*" Her voice sounded happy—not her usual mood.

Jasna opened the door looking wary. "Professor Reid—hi. I'm working on my project at home," she blurted out, as if stumbling too fast down a hill.

"I didn't come to check up on you," Iris reassured her. "I was just wondering if you can tell me some things about Lara. May I come in?"

Jasna stepped back from the doorway. "I saw you on TV Saturday night, what you did at the airport. It was awesome. I can't believe that bastard almost escaped."

"There are still a lot of parts missing in the story." Iris surveyed the small, dark living room. It was a jumble. Two lumpy upholstered chairs faced each other across a coffee table strewn with books and magazines. Clothes were piled up in a corner, probably waiting for a trip to the laundromat.

"Sorry about the mess. I never let anyone come over here."

"No, I'm sorry to intrude. I was hoping you might fill in some gaps in the story about Lara since you two were friends." Iris winced at her use of the past tense.

Jasna glanced nervously around the room, then said. "Have a seat. Would you like some tea?"

"That would be great, thanks."

Jasna disappeared through an arched doorway and Iris heard cabinet doors banging.

She tried to settle in one of the chairs but the sharp end of a broken spring pressed into her, so she stood up and paced slowly around the room instead. She glanced out a window that overlooked the parking lot, then noticed an open laptop on a nearby desk. She looked over quickly toward the arched opening and, hearing the rattle of metal on the stove, she approached and grazed her finger along the top of the touchpad. The background image on the screen stopped her cold. It was the face that had been plastered on posters all over Boston. Same hazel eyes with black lashes. But in this picture, Lara's hair had been cut short and dyed blond. The girl was smiling happily, as if she didn't have a care in the world.

A loud crash made Iris look up. Jasna, standing in the doorway, held an empty tray with broken crockery and a spreading brown puddle of tea at her feet.

They stared at each other in shocked silence.

Iris finally said, "Why do you have this picture of Lara? When was it taken?"

Jasna's eyes flitted around the room. "You have no right,"

she cried out before sinking into a Director's chair. She was on the edge of hysteria and began to mutter in an unintelligable language, shaking her head and moaning. Finally, she switched to English. "You don't know what he did—what he took from me."

Iris took a deep breath and steadied herself. "Then tell me. Explain it to me. Because it looks to me like an innocent man is sitting in jail for a crime that maybe never happened."

Jasna leapt up from her seat, darted toward the desk, and grabbed a large pair of scissors. Iris was quickly on her feet and close behind her. Jasna twisted toward her with the scissors high in the air, hesitated, then collapsed into a chair, letting her weapon clatter to the wood floor. Iris kicked the scissors under a radiator then planted herself across from her student, her heart pounding faster than usual as she reached into her pocket for her cell phone.

"Explain to me now what that picture is doing on your laptop or I'll call the police and you can explain it to them," she said.

"Xander DeWitt is not an innocent man. He raped me," Jasna gulped down tears. "When I was twelve. In Bosnia."

Iris hovered indecisively, then put away her phone and lowered herself to the edge of a chair. "I'm listening."

After a moment, the young woman collected herself enough to start speaking again. "It was thirteen years ago. I was in the woods with my older brother looking for clothing to take off the dead Muslims or anything else we could trade for food. We were starving. I had wandered away from Edvin thinking I saw a bush with berries we could eat."

"A man grabbed me from behind. A soldier. He wrapped his hand over my mouth so I couldn't scream, then dragged me into a shed. He kept me there for three days, leaving me tied up and gagged in the dark at night. I could hear my brother outside calling for me but I couldn't move or make a sound. The soldier would return to rape me again each afternoon. I bit his hand at one point and that drove him into a frenzy." She shuddered. "What happened during those three days ended my childhood. But what DeWitt did to me next ended my belief in God."

"How do you know that this soldier was Xander DeWitt?"

"He was wearing a UN uniform with a nameplate, DeWitt. Oh, and he had a tattoo on his shoulder."

"Where exactly was the tattoo? What did it look like?" Iris asked.

"Here." Jasna pointed to her right shoulder. "It was a butterfly. I would watch the different colors run together as I cried while he was raping me."

Iris covered her mouth with her hand.

"They called themselves Peacekeepers," Jasna went on, "but those so-called soldiers did nothing while the Serbs tried their best to exterminate us. DeWitt was as much a predator as the Serbs themselves. Maybe worse."

Jasna stared blankly at the floor. "On the third day, after he had taken his day's pleasure, he gave me back my clothes. I thought he would let me go then. Instead, he marched me through the woods toward a village where the Serbs had made a camp. He tied me to a tree, and left me there. It took the Serbs less than an hour to find me and to drag me off to one of their rape houses. Do you know what those are?"

"Yes," Iris whispered.

"I was the youngest girl so I was very popular. The older women tried to protect me, but that just earned them more beatings. The war ended several months later, but by that point, I just wanted to die. A woman from my village helped me get home. *Home*. It was never *home* after that. My parents could not look me in the eyes after they learned what had happened." Jasna slowly got up and said, over her shoulder, "Let me show you something."

Iris followed close behind to make sure Jasna wasn't looking for another weapon.

Jasna went to a bookshelf, selected a book and slid

something out from between its pages. She handed Iris an old photograph, dog-eared from frequent handling. It showed a very young Jasna holding a baby. It looked like she was holding her younger sister.

"Was it DeWitt's?"

"How would I know?" Jasna's face had hardened into a mask of bitterness.

Finally Iris asked, "How does all this tie in with the picture of Lara on your laptop?"

Jasna's expression softened. "I named the baby Esmina after my grandmother. I tried to take care of her but, even after the war was over, there was no money, no food. Plus, I was just a child myself, a damaged child."

"My brother came up with an idea. Edvin is gay, and he wanted us to emigrate to a more tolerant country. He decided that we should go to Canada. There was only one problem. We would both need to work full time to earn the money to move us from country to country. I couldn't work while taking care of Esmina. My mother wouldn't take her. But I knew of a nice woman in the next village who couldn't have children of her own. She agreed to raise my baby. It broke my heart to part with Esmina, but I figured I could come back from Canada to visit her once I was settled there. She would have a better childhood with this woman to look out for her."

"It took Edvin and me two years to work our way to Montreal. By that time my mother had written to say that my baby's family had moved away—maybe to the United States, she wasn't sure. Edvin and I lived in a refugee shelter in Montreal for a few years, then were able to get our own apartment. He went to university on a scholarship and got certified as a paramedic."

"I studied hard at the *lycée*, then after a degree from McGill, I got accepted to architecture school. By then, I had gathered up enough money to hire a private investigator to track down Esmina's family. I couldn't believe my luck when, not so long ago, the P.I. tracked them down to Cambridge."

"So Lara is your daughter," Iris said, having already guessed it.

"Yes. I watched her for many days, then approached her at her father's store six months ago. We became friends but I didn't tell her who I was. The woman I'd given her to, the woman Lara thought of as her mother, had died a few years ago. Her brute of a husband was intending to ship Lara back to Bosnia this summer to marry some crony of his. Lara was terrified."

"I knew I had to get her to someplace safe and keep her

father from finding her. Edvin and his partner said they'd be glad to raise her in Montreal until I graduated from architecture school. I would see her on holidays and we would Skype every day. By then GSD had started fall semester and I'd seen him—the man who'd destroyed my life. I hadn't realized he'd become a famous architect until I saw him here, making his big presentation."

"Why didn't you try to expose him then? You could have told everyone what he had done to you."

"Who would have believed me? I'm just a lowly architecture student, invisible. In this world he's a god. Everyone admires him."

"So you figured out a way to get your revenge. What did you do next?"

Jasna slid off her wire-rimmed glasses, cleaned the lenses with the hem of her sweatshirt, then put them back on. "I sent Lara off with my brother. That's all I know."

"You're lying. Tell me how you set it all up. Every step or I go to the police."

Jasna's knuckles were white as she gripped the arms of the chair. Long seconds passed. Finally she continued. "I instructed Lara to go to his office, to ask directions first so someone would see her there. I knew DeWitt was teaching a studio then, so there was no danger he would see her. I also knew she'd be escaping to safety in Montreal soon afterward. I figured if people said Lara had been there to see DeWitt before she disappeared maybe the police would look into his past."

Jasna stopped speaking and stared out the window.

"Keep going. Tell me everything."

"I had cut and dyed Lara's hair the night she went missing. That was the evening I told her I was her mother." Jasna flicked away the tear rolling down her cheek. She collected herself and continued. "Edvin drove down here to pick her up. I'd found some car keys when I broke into DeWitt's house."

"Wait—you're the one who broke into Xander's house?"

Jasna gave her an impatient look. "The keys were labeled with the neighbor's house number, so we borrowed the van for the drive to Manchester as another link to DeWitt. I knew from his GSD lecture that he'd gone there recently, so that's where we planted the clues—making prints with his boots and leaving my bedspread. Edvin, as a trained paramedic, told me how to collect Lara's blood. That part was hard. I had to collect her blood many times to get enough."

"We made the trail lead right to DeWitt, figuring the police would look deeper into his background, maybe find out about his dirty little secrets. When I was in his house earlier I'd even downloaded some disgusting porn of young girls to his computer, hoping the police would find it."

"Was the guy from your apartment in on your plan?"

"Mark?" Jasna shook her head. "No, he didn't have a clue what was going on. He's out there every night with the baby, so Edvin drove the van right by him. Mark's got a photographic memory. I figured he'd get most of the license plate right."

"Why did you draw me into it? You came to my house asking for help."

"The police weren't picking up the trail. They suspected the father. I needed to get the police to find the van. Besides, you'd given DeWitt an alibi. I needed you to doubt his innocence."

"Wait a minute. How did you know I provided an alibi for DeWitt?"

For the first time, Jasna looked sheepish. "I'd followed him on that Friday after the initial presentations. I knew you two were out at dinner so I'd have time to break in. I wanted to see if there were e-mails between you two so I could learn what he was up to. And, sorry to say, you left your laptop right on my desk. It didn't take long to drop in some spyware so I could monitor your mail. You talked to your brother about your alibi for DeWitt."

"So that's why you bugged my computer. And you continued

to spy on my e-mails. You invaded my privacy," Iris snapped.

"And you invaded mine by opening my laptop," Jasna snapped right back.

They stared at each other until Iris broke the silence. "I guess invasion of privacy is the least of the issues on the table now. You've created a setup for DeWitt that will probably get him convicted of kidnapping and murder. The *Globe* is saying he might even get the death penalty."

"Don't you think he deserves to die?" Jasna asked.

CHAPTER 63

Jasna leaned against the door frame and listened to Iris Reid's steps retreating down the staircase. Iris had given her a twenty-four hour reprieve before she would take any action so she could think carefully about what was fair.

Fair? Was it fair that, after everything she and Edvin had risked, the fate of her daughter might rest in the hands of Iris Reid?

Jasna had pointed out that since Lara's adoptive father was in prison for trying to kill DeWitt, if Iris were to alert the authorities to the fact that Lara was alive, the poor girl would be returned to Massachusetts and placed in a foster home. Wasn't it better for Lara to be able to finish her teenaged years with her biological mother and the uncle who loved her? Jasna had pleaded with Iris to let DeWitt be punished, even if it were for the wrong crime.

Jasna closed the door and sank into the nearest chair. She would need to call Edvin to discuss the possibility of triggering Plan B. She hated the idea that she and Edvin would have to uproot their lives yet again, but she knew that he was as determined as she was to prevent their newly united family from being torn apart.

She was blessed to have a brother like Edvin. He was willing to move to France with her if that would keep them all together. The two siblings had each kept their dual French and Canadian citizenship, the former earned during their slow emigrant crawl to Montreal. They'd been only too happy to shed any allegiance to wretched Bosnia. Edvin had researched the law—France would not allow the extradition of its own citizens back to the U.S. to face bogus charges of kidnapping their own daughter and niece.

Jasna knew that she had to keep looking ahead, not behind. If Iris decided to expose their ruse, Jasna could still enact as much of the plan as possible, if she moved quickly enough. She wouldn't give up the satisfaction of seeing DeWitt piece together the fact that she was the one framing him. She was not helpless this time.

Her skin felt too tight, too tight. *Do it. Release the pain.* She drifted into her small bedroom and over to the wooden box she kept on the window sill. Jasna took out the X-ACTO knife and studied its razor-sharp point. This would be the last time she would cut herself. Feeling anything, even pain, meant that she was still alive.

Jasna slipped off her jeans and climbed up onto the bed. She looked down at the highway of scars crisscrossing her thighs. She followed a track with her finger as tears spilled down her cheeks. She loved seeing the first spurt of red blood against her white skin.

CHAPTER 64

Xander tasted a trickle of blood oozing out of his split lip as a guard led him toward the visiting room. When he had agreed to put this student on his approved visitor list, he had anticipated the meeting as a welcome distraction from the endless battery of questions the prison pyschiatrist kept asking him. He and his roommate, The Ram, were getting along fine after their initial scuffle. Xander had gotten Nils to make a contribution to The Ram's prison bank account in order to forestall any further sexual advances. Now The Ram was on his payroll as a bodyguard. Some of the cruder inmates referred to Xander as "The Ram's bitch," but at least they left him alone.

Who was this student coming to see him? There was no "Jasna" in his studio group. She had said she was a second year GSD student who had followed his career, but she'd been mysterious about why she wanted to see him. Probably wanted career advice. Even inside a prison he couldn't get away from people desiring him as a mentor. He looked down at his gray sweatsuit. It didn't look bad on his trim physique. Gray had always been a good color for him, far better than neon orange. He just wished the guard would remove his handcuffs. It was hard to look dignified in handcuffs.

They passed through a second sally port, waiting as one set of doors whumped shut, followed by a second set clicking open. After a turn in the corridor, a side wall opened into a glass panel embedded with chicken wire. Through the panel he could see a large room separated into small cubicles, with formica tables separating inmates from visitors.

He was led into one of the cubicles and he regarded the young woman on the other side. Not a flicker of recognition illuminated him. He sat down on a chair bolted to the floor and rested his hands in his lap.

"Hello," he said, a question in his voice.

"It's been a long time," she said.

"Have we met?"

"How does it feel to be the one in the cage this time?"

Xander stared at her, struck by her words. "Pardon?"

"I'm disappointed. There's an expression—'you always remember your first,' but I guess it was just my first time, not yours. I know I've changed. It's been a long time since we were 'together' in Bosnia. Do you still have that butterfly tattoo on your shoulder or doesn't it suit your present image?"

There was silence. The student's flaring eyes became transformed in his memory into the huge eyes of an innocent waif. He could picture her lithe body. "Impossible," he whispered. He leaned forward to see her better. "You're alive?"

The girl's face was white as bone. "Despite your best efforts."

Her angry words wounded him. "No, no, precious girl. You misunderstood. I tried to protect you. But the war wouldn't let us be together. I had to let you go and it's been the biggest regret of my life. There's never been anyone else like you."

She leaned close and whispered in his ear. "You're a sick man. I want you to know that it's been me who's spun this web around you. And because of me you'll be in this cage until the day you die."

CHAPTER 65

Iris rested her cheek against the cool glass of her turreted office window. The light had begun to soften into dusk. A roller suitcase clicked loudly from outside as it was wheeled along the brick sidewalk. She gazed out at pedestrians rushing up the block to the warmth and safety of their homes and felt as though she inhabited a different universe, one in which twelve-year-old girls got dragged off to rape houses and nobody cared.

She returned to her desk and collapsed into the adjustable chair. Her mind had been spinning for hours with Jasna's story, touching down fitfully on each instance of wrongs committed and to whom, weighing each awful offense. How could it ever be put right? How could Iris' abiding need for truth be so at odds with her equally powerful need for fairness?

She couldn't talk this over with Ellie. Luc had walked away. This was her own damn ethical burden to unravel. Hadn't she told Jasna that she, Iris Reid, would decide what the next step in this story would be? But what right did she have to be the judge? At least three people's lives—Lara's, Jasna's and Xander's—could be critically affected by whatever action she might choose.

Nonetheless, Iris marveled at how clever the plan was. From Jasna arranging for Lara to visit Xander's office, to breaking into Xander's house, to setting up a fake but gruesome murder scene in that New Hampshire barn. Her student was inspired—Iris had to give her that. The whole intricate setup would punish Xander, with the secondary benefit of getting Lara's father to stop looking for the girl.

But then Iris stopped and remembered that part of this oh-so-ingenious plan involved Jasna's reading Iris' private e-mails, spying on Iris' account for weeks. Jasna had also used Iris to lead the police to the van. Maybe Jasna was still conning her. Maybe she hadn't been raped. No, to Iris that part of the story sounded real. Why else would Jasna go to this much trouble to pursue revenge against Xander? Iris could no longer think of him as the dedicated architect who had taken her out to dinner six weeks before and shown such interest in her work. Now she could only imagine him as a depraved, manipulative pedophile.

Still, he hadn't killed Lara. He'd never even met her. Iris had always felt proud that the American justice system at least attempted to follow strict rules about culpability. Wouldn't that make her a vigilante, or at least an accessory to one, if she let Jasna get away with sending Xander to prison, or worse, to a date with the executioner?

Lara was the only innocent one here. She was now safe from her bully of an adoptive father and was presumably living happily with her uncle. Shouldn't she be left alone? Iris had no illusions about how Lara's life would be as a ward of the state.

Blissfully unaware of her mistress' anxiety, Sheba padded into the office and looked at Iris expectantly, tail wagging.

With a sigh, Iris rose and went through the doorway into the kitchen, flipping on the lights. She poured kibble into Sheba's battered, stainless steel bowl. She retrieved some last pieces of leftover chicken from the fridge, arranged it on top of the kibble and returned the bowl to its spot by the back door. Sheba sauntered over to it, sniffing the air.

Noting the time on the microwave, Iris rummaged in the refrigerator for her own dinner. She ended up eating two bowls of Cheerios. As she ate, she watched the evening news on her laptop. The leading story was about a journalist who'd been captured in

Iraq months before. He was shown holding up a recent newspaper, presumably to prove that he was still alive.

Iris chewed distractedly and thought.

CHAPTER 66

Xander had wasted no time in calling his solicitor. Thus, on Wednesday, the morning after Jasna's visit, he sat across from Farrington and the solicitor's younger colleague in a depressing cell that passed for an interview room at Walpole Prison.

"You're saying that the perpetrator of this hoax came to see you and admitted to everything?" Farrington's bright dark eyes were fixed intently on Xander.

"Yes, like I told you on the phone, she showed up here yesterday and said that she was the reason I was in prison. It's a girl I had, let us say, a dalliance with in Bosnia. She is out for revenge because things did not, uh—I wasn't very good with splitting up."

The younger attorney, Martin-something, paused from taking notes on his iPad, then asked "Was this the woman you said might be Lara's mother?"

DeWitt felt a moment of panic, then shook away the possibility. "No, this is a different one. You need to see the tape of our interview. You can hear what she says. This place records all the visits, don't they?"

Farrington's lips tightened into a slit. "The warden already showed us the tape of your interview with this Jasna Sidron. Her words are not very clear, especially at the end. We checked on her identity when you called yesterday afternoon and she really is a GSD student."

"You can interview her." Xander said. "In any case, now we know who is behind all of this. The police can check on her movements. She must have made some mistakes. Lara must be hidden away somewhere."

"Here's the problem," Farrington said, frowning. "We can't hear her saying anything incriminating on the tape."

"But can't technicians do things to make the words easier to hear? I thought there were all kinds of—"

Farrington interrupted him. "Yes, we can try to enhance the sound, but you're missing the inherent problem with telling a jury that she's the one setting you up. They'll want to know why she's so eager for revenge. Her student visa says she is twenty-five years old. You were in Bosnia thirteen, fourteen years ago, yes? This girl would have been eleven or twelve then. Are you telling us you had sex with a girl of that age?"

"Sex?" Xander looked away. "No, not really sex. It was more of a crush she had on me. I was more of a mentor to her, I guess. Then my commission ended and I left. She must have been angry that I didn't stay in touch."

"So, if we had this young lady on the witness stand, is that the story she would tell?" Farrington gave Xander a dry look. "Because if, instead, she would say that you forced yourself on her in Bosnia when she was the same age as Lara—the jury is just going to see a pattern of sexual abuse of a minor going back over a dozen years. This could make your case worse."

"But how can the truth that I'm being set up make my case worse?" Xander asked.

"We were always planning on raising the idea that you had been set up. But to say that the person behind it is another young lady whom you might have harmed when she was the same age as Lara—it's not a good strategy for gaining sympathy."

"But I have never even met Lara! I didn't hurt her! Are you saying that now that we know who set me up, we can't use that information to get me out of here?"

"We'll enhance the tape to see if there's anything that will benefit your case." Farrington said.

The solicitors stood up and collected their files.

"Maybe we can find a way to spin this," Farrington added as he headed toward the door and rapped on the glass.

CHAPTER 67

Jasna chewed on her lower lip as she paced around her apartment, cell phone cradled on her shoulder.

"Holding a copy of *The Boston Globe*? Where am I supposed to get that in Montreal?" Edvin asked, zeroing in on one of many complicated details of the plan.

"I could overnight one to you," Jasna replied. "We just need a paper that won't give away where Lara is now and it needs to be somewhat recent to show that Lara is still alive and well."

"Did you agree to this? It unravels everything we put together."

Jasna sighed. "I know—I screwed up. I let my professor into the apartment and she saw Lara's photo on my laptop. Now we're stuck having Iris Reid dictate what we have to do. Our only other option is to make a run for France."

"And if we don't do what she says she goes to the police and turns you in? I thought you said you could trust her."

"Listen—her solution acomplishes our goal. We take the photo but it won't be released to the press until DeWitt admits what he did to me in Bosnia. We'll have Lara safe with us. Her father's locked up so he can't come hunting for her. You can photograph her against a white backdrop so no one can figure out where she is. And I don't get prosecuted or kicked out of the country for setting up DeWitt, for sending him porn, for breaking into his house, or for spying on my professor's e-mails."

"No one was supposed to be able to tie any of this to us."

"Well, that horse escaped from the barn, or whatever the expression is. Anyway, DeWitt's spent some time in jail, even gotten roughed up judging from the cuts on his face. After he's released from custody here he may just get hauled up in front of the World Court in the Hague for war crimes. His career is already destroyed."

"When you put it that way, I guess it does sound like enough."

"Nothing will ever be enough. I'll get my degree and return to Montreal so we can all be a family. That's the most important thing."

"You're right, little sister. Keeping our family together and safe is worth more than revenge."

CHAPTER 68

Two days later, Xander sat again in the same interview room with Farrington and Martin- something.

"You said on the phone there had been a development?" Xander asked.

"Martin and I had an interesting chat with Jasna Sidran yesterday. She wants to make a deal with you," Farrington said.

"What kind of a deal?"

"Ms. Sidran said that she would produce a photograph showing Lara holding up a recent copy of a newspaper to establish that the girl is still alive."

"That's great! That would get me out of here, yes?" Xander looked hopefully at his solicitors and wondered why they looked so stony faced. A bit more slowly he asked, "In exchange for what?"

"You would have to admit that when you were a peacekeeper in Bosnia you raped the twelve-year-old Ms. Sidran." Farrington said.

Xander sat up straight. "But it wasn't like that. We were in a relationship."

"She was twelve years old," Farrington practically shouted. "You were in a position of power, wearing a peacekeeper's uniform. That was NOT a relationship."

Martin raised a hand placatingly. "Regardless of how you viewed matters, Ms. Sidran is adamant that, in exchange for the photograph, you must admit to your guilt."

After several minutes of staring at the scarred table, Xander coughed lightly. "What would the implications be if I did that?"

Martin consulted his iPad before speaking. "It's highly likely that the D.A. would drop the case against you. As for the admitted rape in Bosnia, the UN has left punishment for what it deems to be sexual exploitation by its peacekeepers to the individual countries to prosecute. Typical punishments have run from reduction in military rank to eight months in prison. Often there is no punishment, especially after so many years have elapsed."

Xander ran a hand through his hair. How had the girl

outsmarted him? Even the better option would be unpleasant. "So, in any case, I'd be free of this prison nightmare to go back home to Holland. But I'd be disgraced in most people's eyes."

Farrington inspected his fingernails while Martin stared at his iPad screen intently.

"How do we know she would keep her side of the deal?" Xander asked.

"She wants you to make your statement to William Buchanan of *The Boston Globe,*" Farrington said. "After your admission gets printed in *The Globe,* she says she will release the photograph to the same reporter."

"But what if she is lying? Can you make her give you the photograph beforehand to hold onto, to make sure that it actually exists before I stick my neck out?"

Farrington shook his head. "As attorneys we're officers of the court. We'd be bound to turn over evidence like that immediately to the D.A. I doubt Ms. Sidron would agree to let that happen before she sees your admission in print."

"But then we have no leverage," Xander said. "I'd be a fool to trust this girl to keep her word after what she's done to me."

Farrington looked thoughtful. "Maybe's there's some neutral

party who would agree to act as a go-between."

Martin looked up from typing notes. "What about having Iris Reid hold onto the photo? She's Ms. Sidran's professor. Isn't she someone you trust, Professor DeWitt?"

CHAPTER 69

Xander slid his cafeteria tray along the shelf, regarding the day's offerings with dismay. What kind of meat was in a sloppy joe? Why was it orange? Did he even want to know?

The Ram stood at his side, as he always did in public areas. He took his bodyguard duties seriously, as well he should for the extortionate amount Nils had deposited into his bank account.

Xander resignedly pointed to a cheese sandwich and the pimply, hairnetted server lifted his spatula.

"Get another one of those," The Ram instructed. The prison-dictated limits on food left the man constantly hungry.

After Xander waggled two fingers, he watched the rubbery bread being flopped onto a plate. Between his distaste for prison food and the free-weight workouts, he'd be down to sinew and bone in no time and able to fit into his tightest bespoke suits.

Ignoring countless staring eyes, Xander waited for The Ram to finish loading up his tray before the two steered toward an empty table in the corner. The background clatter of the kitchen and men's low voices jangled his nerves. It was never quiet in prison. If it wasn't doors clanging, or guards shouting, it was constant announcements on the PA system.

"You meetin' with those lawyers again this afternoon?" the Ram asked, his mouth full of sloppy joe.

"No, a reporter."

The Ram did a double take. "This the guy from *The Globe* who keeps calling you a perv?"

"That's the one. Only this time *I* will be telling *him* what to write." *And it will get me out of this hellhole.*

"Good luck with that."

Instead of engineering an escape, was he walking into a trap? As he sat chewing the tasteless cheese whiz sandwich, the girl's words echoed in his head. "I want you to know that it's been me who's spun this web around you."

Why did she seem to hate him? Or was this an elaborate plan to worm her way back into his life? Maybe she had been as haunted by their encounter as he had been—the excitement, the danger, the sensual thrill. Still, it was a strange way of getting his attention. His solicitors had warned him not to call what they had shared a relationship, and, in all fairness, it hadn't been that. It was a stolen few days that had changed his life. It had showed him who he really was. It must have changed her life, too.

"Because of me you'll be in this cage until the day you die." Weren't love and hate two sides of the same coin? Hadn't she reversed course and offered him a way out of the cage several days later?

Xander pushed away his tray and leaned back in his plastic chair. Why was her price for his freedom having to say he'd raped her? Such an ugly word. She must want him to prove that he was willing to degrade himself for her. The fleeting image of leaving the girl tied to a tree rose up in his memory, but he submerged it immediately. That was not part of the narrative. He had done what he had to do to survive. It was a war, after all.

But he was left with the question of what she wanted from him after he got out. Of course he would return to Europe as fast as he could flee from this uncivilized continent. Did she think she could be a part of his life now? With a shudder, he realized he might have to spell it out for her that she was no longer his type. She was well past that golden moment when a girl stands on the edge of womanhood.

The Ram helped himself to Xander's last sandwich as Xander consulted the wall clock. Five more minutes until lunch was over.

How long before he'd be savoring the Cacio e Pepe pasta with a bracing glass of Vermantino on the outdoor terrace of Palladio in Amsterdam? How long before the doting architectural critics again begged for interviews about his work? Sure, some notoriety would follow him from this experience. But people would forget soon enough. A little danger might even add to his allure.

Xander drank a carton of milk and blotted his mouth with a paper napkin.

Time to meet with Robert Buchanan.

CHAPTER 70

Iris barely registered the Mozart concerto playing quietly in the background as she stared at the printed rendering of the front of the guest house. Something bothered her about the front facade. Even though the GSD design committee had signed off on her design development plans and elevations, Iris still wasn't satisfied. The drawings needed to be submitted to the Harvard Square Historical Commission soon, so if she was going to make any changes, they needed to be made now.

She propped the print up on the tilted drafting board section of her enormous desk and stood back a few feet. Now that Iris' design had been translated from her original hand-drawn sketches to CAD drawings, her sense that something was missing had increased. She had abstracted some of the elements of the adjacent brick building that housed *The Crimson,* the University's student paper. She had designed some of the bricks on her building to be pulled out and turned ninety degrees to create decorative string courses while other areas of brick were indented to create panels. The composition of planes and pattern, while not symmetrical, balanced harmoniously. She'd have to convince the Historical Commission that this modern interpretation of a Georgian building was appropriate for the precious environment of Harvard Square. Somehow the egg crate design of Holyoke Center across the street had gotten through their approval process. Or maybe that had slipped through the net before the Commission was formed.

The trill of her landline interrupted her thoughts.

"Iris, W.T.F.!" a man's voice shouted.

"Who is this?"

"It's Bobby—Budge. Did you know what DeWitt was going to confess to me today?"

"Did he admit to taking Lara?"

"Don't play dumb with me. You're in this up to your eyeballs. DeWitt tells me you're supposed to hand over something to me— the second part of the story, so let's cut to the chase. I want the whole thing now before I write this up. I don't want to end up with egg on my face."

"If I'm supposed to do something, it's news to me. What did DeWitt tell you?"

"What's the spin you two are aiming for?"

"Who the hell knows? I'm the one who kept him from escaping at Logan—remember? Now you're telling me he expects me to be his accomplice? I'm not sure I want any part of this."

"Fine—if you won't be straight with me you can read about DeWitt's bombshell in *The Globe* tomorrow along with the rest of our lucky readers."

"I can hardly wait."

Iris picked up the thumb drive containing Lara's photo from the desk and held it in the palm of her hand. It felt so light. She sighed and slipped it into a green glass cup on her bookshelf.

CHAPTER 71

Iris had always loved the annual Honk festival. That Sunday afternoon, she snapped on Sheba's leash, slipped the thumb drive and some cash into the pocket of her jeans, and wandered down Arlington Street toward Mass Ave. The parade had already started at Davis Square in Somerville, the neighboring town, and was wending its way past Iris' neighborhood. The various activist street bands, like Grannies Against War, and the Vocal Majority, joined with dancers and assorted revelers to converge in Harvard Square at an all-purpose Oktoberfest celebration.

Iris stopped at Ellie's house and rang the doorbell. Her friend flew out the door wearing a purple wig and a pink tutu over her leggings.

"Are you part of the parade?" Iris asked.

"Just showing my support," Ellie said from a crouch as she tied a glittery bow onto Sheba's collar.

They continued arm in arm down Arlington Street. They

could hear the parade music from half a block away. As they reached the throngs of people assembled on the sidewalks along Mass Ave, they merged into the crowd and watched the spectacle pass by.

"Look, there are the fire-eaters," Ellie called out, pointing.

Eight men and women in striped costumes spit flaming lighter fluid onto rings that they held up high as the crowd oohed and aahed. They swung the rings around in bright arcs.

Iris found herself swaying to the rhythm of the blasting horns and pounding drums, then noticed Sheba attentively watching a cyclist in a Dr. Seuss costume ride by, towing a tiny dog on an even tinier float. Next, Iris spotted their seventy-year-old neighbor, Alise, decked out in a feathery cape, shaking a tambourine. Iris waved to her and Alise raised her instrument in reply. Children in bright yellow costumes with faces painted in peace symbols marched by, twirling colorful flags. A passing group sporting multi-colored dreadlocks belted out gospel songs.

"I think they're from New Orleans," Ellie yelled above the din.

After twenty minutes of the unfolding extravaganza, Iris touched Ellie's arm and said, "I'm going to head down to Harvard Square."

"See you later," Ellie yelled back. "I'm going home soon. Some writing to finish."

Iris and Sheba followed the brilliant pageant down Mass Ave and into the labyrinth of Harvard Square. Food booths featuring dishes from around the world lined the sidewalks. Iris stopped to buy a nice fat bratwurst, then tore off several pieces to share with Sheba. She proceeded to finish the rest of it while watching a troupe of Chinese dancers in flowing dragon costumes on the main stage, set up in The Pit, one of the triangular corners of Harvard Square which, like all of the Squares in Cambridge, was not actually rectangular.

When her ears started to ring, she headed toward the Charles River on the far southwest side of the Square. The crowd thinned as she approached the Larz Anderson Bridge. She walked up to the center of the bridge and stared down into the murky water below, with the skyline of Boston in the distance. An eight-seat rowing shell emerged from under the bridge, headed downstream with its coxswain calling out strokes, barely audible as they sped away.

Sheba sat at her feet watching her mistress. Iris reached in her pocket and felt the thumb drive. She thought again about the awful disconnect between truth and fairness.

Then she heard his voice.

"Tell me why we had to meet here, Reid. What are we, Cold War spies?"

Budge.

CHAPTER 72

Russo had dropped off his son, Charlie Jr., at school on his way to work. The eleven-year- old was disgusted by the new restrictions on his usual freedom to roam the neighborhood, but his detective father was not taking any chances with someone grabbing his kid.

Now, at nine-fifteen on a Monday morning, he and Malone stood before the murder board staring at the photo of the familiar young face, cut out from that morning's front page of *The Globe*.

"D'you think it was photo-shopped?" Russo said, rubbing the back of his neck.

"The original's just passed our techies, and it passed *The Globe's* vetters. I think we have to assume it's real."

"After all the blood we found in New Hampshire, how can she still be alive? How can that be possible?"

"The ME says if it was extracted in small enough amounts over time— she could've survived," Malone said.

"So this was all a hoax. Why? And who?" Russo voice was getting loud.

"Not DeWitt evidently. But he did admit to the reporter that he raped a young girl in Bosnia. So now he's branded as a pedophile plus his reputation is shot, if he cares."

"I don't get it. Why would DeWitt admit to a crime so far in his past? Did he have some reason to think it was going to come out?"

"We can't get anything out of his lawyers. Maybe the guy's had a jailhouse conversion and he wants to get it off his chest. He still claims he had nothing to do with Lara." Malone sank down into a chair. "I wouldn't be surprised if his admission was part of a deal he made, so the photo showing Lara alive would surface and he'd get off on the charge of kidnap and murder."

Russo walked closer to the photograph. "Who would benefit from pretending the girl was taken? Can we trace anything from the photo? What's in the background?"

Malone put on his reading glasses and peered closely at the picture. "Looks like a sheet but it's blurry. It'll be tough for the techies to pull out any context that might show where Lara is now."

"She looks happy enough though. That's one thing to be glad

about. Do we know where the hell that reporter got the photo?"

"Iris Reid gave it to him. She claimed she got an envelope through her mail slot containing the thumb drive and instructions to pass it on to Buchanan."

"Iris Reid—again?"

"I'm having Carter bring her in for a little conversation."

CHAPTER 73

Iris wondered how many times she was going to get called into this same police interview room. Stale and drab though it was, it was beginning to feel like home. Sterling sat next to her, a loud argyle sock exposed as he jiggled an ankle over his knee.

Malone and Russo filed in, the former flipping on the wall switch for the recording system, the latter naming the room's occupants in a clear, unemotional tone.

Malone began. "Ms. Reid, we understand you passed along a photograph to Robert Buchanan of *The Boston Globe* this past Sunday afternoon. Where did you get it?"

Sterling gave her a tiny nod and Iris reached into her purse and handed over a manila envelope addressed to Robert Buchanan care of Iris Reid in block letters.

"This was put through my mail slot. I didn't see who left it."

Iris hoped that Jasna had been careful about fingerprints. She explained that Budge Buchanan was an old college friend and she had figured the package was some information for a story. She had opened the envelope but hadn't looked at what was on the thumb drive. She assumed now that it was the picture of Lara that *The Globe* had printed that morning. Sterling nudged her foot under the table and Iris stopped speaking.

After an hour of rephrased questions and circuitous conversation, the detectives still hadn't been able to shake Iris' story that she had no idea who had dropped off the envelope. They let her go.

*   *   *

A week later, Iris' office phone rang.

"Martin Taylor just called," Sterling confided. "Great guy. Class behind me at Yale Law. You didn't tell me he was representing DeWitt."

"And great-guy Martin called you because...?"

"We were setting up a squash game and he mentioned that the D.A.'s dropping the case against DeWitt. Their evidence was always circumstantial, but with DeWitt's attorneys now waving the photo of Lara in front of the cameras, it's become too much of a stretch. I heard from Martin that DeWitt's getting on a plane to Amsterdam tomorrow."

Iris took a minute to let that reality sink in. "I wonder what will happen to his career. Are clients going to want to associate with him?"

"Depends on the client. He's still a brilliant architect."

"And a despicable human being."

"That's never stopped people from climbing the ladder to fame and glory."

Iris felt hollow at the thought. "I can't believe this Lara saga is finally over."

"Now your job is to stay out of trouble. I don't want any more of your phone calls from Cambridge Police Headquarters."

"I'll keep my head down. Thanks for telling me the news."

Iris ended the call and refocused on her drawing. A razor-point pen had rolled to a stopping place halfway across the front elevation. Iris stared. The crossways slash of the pen's barrel broke the perfect balance of the facade. She unrolled a length of yellow tracing paper over the drawing and sketched a new diagonal glass canopy across the building's front. It felt as if she'd just picked the tumblers on a safe, and the heavy door cracked open.

She examined this change from all angles. Finding that she liked the slight friction between the solid and transparent elements, a new movement between parts, she set about adjusting the CAD drawings on her computer. Iris was lost in her work until the daylight in her office began to soften and dim, with a deep pink glow in the western sky.

CHAPTER 74

The next morning, a paralegal from Farrington's office, driving the office Lexus, dropped Xander off at the Howland Street house. The first thing he did was spend a blissful twenty minutes in a hot shower, all by himself. Then, in his silk boxer briefs, Xander set to work packing up his possessions, muttering and cursing as he did so. He had expected Nils to have taken care of this, but the day before, the ungrateful underling had texted Xander his resignation—from both the firm and, most irritatingly, as his personal assistant. Xander had just noticed the message on his laptop when he had scrolled through the hundreds of e-mails that had accumulated, a good portion of them abusive.

After his two navy blue T. Anthony suitcases and a matching briefcase were properly lined up by the front door, Xander changed into the suit he had laid out on the bed. He secured a pair of understated gold cuff links in his French cuffs before sliding on his favorite charcoal Armani jacket and carefully arranging a bright, perfectly folded square handkerchief in the breast pocket.

During the twenty minute taxi ride through the scruffy Somerville streets to Logan Airport, he tried not to think about his last trip along this same route. All of that was now behind him. He could finally return to his real life.

Two glasses of better-than-mediocre champagne in the KLM lounge later, Xander strode toward his seat in the front of the plane. The business class rows were set out as three sets of two seats, and in the seat next to his sat an unappealing, plump teenaged girl with braces, wearing a set of Glow earbuds. She barely registered his presence as he squeezed around her to take his window seat. Xander shook open his *International New York Times,* scanned the familiar articles, and became immersed in the crossword puzzle. Although the language of the clues was so close to his native Dutch in many ways, the inventiveness of the puzzle creators was always a challenge to him.

When Xander glanced up to mull over a particularly tricky clue, he noticed a couple sitting across the aisle from the girl, most likely her parents. The woman, blond with eyes set too far apart, looked over at him and immediately froze. She turned toward her husband and began whispering. The man, large and well-tailored, stood up and tapped his daughter's shoulder.

"Come move to my seat, Amy," he hissed through clenched teeth, as his wife quickly bustled off toward the galley.

The startled girl took out her earbuds and opened her mouth to complain, but her father grabbed her arm and hoisted her up.

Amy stared at Xander, pegging him as the source of her father's concern, then gathered her magazines from the seatback and relocated to her father's seat with a beleaguered sigh.

A stout flight attendant with a fixed smile marched out of the galley toward Xander, followed with some apparent energy by Amy's mother. The other passengers were beginning to look up from their cocktails to watch the scene curiously.

"Mr. DeWitt, there seems to be some confusion with your seat assignment," the flight attendant said. "Would you please come back with me to the galley so we can straighten this out?"

Xander held up his boarding pass, but the attendant nonetheless gave him a follow-me-now gesture.

"Please wait right here sir while I speak with the captain," she said, leaving Xander squeezed between stainless steel carts and the tiny door to the restroom. By now, everyone in the business class section was looking at him with varying degrees of interest. Several of the passengers whispered to each other. Xander tried to maintain his dignity as he stood on full, unwelcome display.

Five minutes later, the flight attendant reappeared. "Mr. DeWitt, your seat is broken, I'm afraid. You'll have to move to the back. We do have an empty seat in Row 5."

She steered him past the other staring passengers to a corner seat as far away from #1A as possible while still credibly within the business class compartment. The seat next to him was empty. The man sitting across the aisle gave him a burning glare before ducking back into his book.

While the plane taxied down the runway, waited in queue, then finally took off, Xander stewed about this sorry treatment. Is this what his life would be like from now on—being treated like a pariah? Surely it would be different in Europe. Europeans weren't such awful, judgmental Puritans. He focused his thoughts on being back in his office, guiding his grateful disciples on their projects and issuing orders that would be quickly followed.

After the seatbelt light was finally turned off, Xander opened his laptop and composed a letter to his partner, Stefan, telling him that the whole American fiasco had been straightened out, and that he was now en route to Amsterdam. He would be back in the office the next day to once again assume the helm of Co-op dWa.

Xander set his laptop on the empty seat next to him and went back to his crossword puzzle. Five minutes later, he heard the chime of an incoming e-mail.

Stefan had responded: *Didn't your solicitor give you our notice? Your partnership in Co-op dWa was terminated two days ago after your confession of rape while in Bosnia appeared in all the international papers. You've violated the firm's morals clause. Since this will seriously impact our ability to attract new clients and keep present clients, we must regrettably sever all ties with you, effective immediately.*

Stefan hadn't signed it, as if he couldn't wait even a few seconds longer to sever ties with his long-time partner.

Xander stared at the screen for a long moment, stunned, before a tear escaped and ran down his cheek.

CHAPTER 75

The clang of the mail slot shutting brought Sheba racing on her stubby legs to the entry hall. Iris thought about ignoring what was probably another Greenpeace brochure, but Sheba was practically levitating with excitement.

"I'm coming, I'm coming," she muttered.

As Iris approached the front door, she saw a reprinted page lying face up on the floor, no doubt an announcement for another ethnic restaurant in Porter Square.

"It's just junk mail, Sheba. Chill!"

But Sheba kept sniffing the paper with great interest.

Iris reached down to snatch the circular but Sheba pinned it under her paw and gave her mistress an accusatory look.

Sliding the paper out from under the dog's weight, Iris barely glanced at it before bringing it back to her office and tossing it in her waste paper basket.

Sheba barked.

"Seriously?" she asked the dog. "You consider that worthy of a treat? I don't call that bringing mail to the kitchen."

Sheba barked again.

"I give up." Iris said, raising both hands. "You win."

She retrieved a rolled chicken treat from Sheba's drawer in the adjacent kitchen and placed it on the floor in front of the dog. Sheba ignored it and waddled back to the wastepaper basket and sat down. She barked again.

Iris lifted out the flyer. "Is this what you want?"

Giving it a second look, she noticed an embossed seal in one corner and words that she recognized as Italian. It looked like a copy of an official document. She brought it into the living room and perched on the sofa to study it. Two names were placed on their own lines: Luc Alain Cormier and Giovanna Isobel Pagani. Then she noticed a word that was easy to translate: divorzio.

The page slid out of Iris' hand as she ran out the front door and looked up and down Washington Avenue, Sheba at her heels, sniffing the air.

Iris scanned the backs of the few pedestrians visible from her elevated front porch and, half a block away, spotted Luc's blond head. Sheba tore off at full speed in that direction.

Iris grabbed Sheba's leash from a hook in the entryway and raced off after them.

ACKNOWLEDGMENTS

The characters in Facade bear no resemblance to actual people I know, although I would like to think they would blend in nicely in my Cambridge neighborhood or at Harvard's Graduate School of Design. Some beloved Cambridge places mentioned in the book do exist, although, regrettably, not the Paradise Café.

I would like to thank Lee Lofland and his remarkable Writer's Police Academy for the instructive four days I spent there learning about all the latest tools in the crime fighter's arsenal.

Special thanks go to my esteemed beta reader, Zenith Gross, whose keen insight into the characters kept me on the right path.

For her editing expertise, my deep gratitude goes to Anne Wagner. I promise to keep a copy of the Chicago Manual of Style at hand during the writing of the next book.

This book is far richer for the prodding and inspiration of my writing group extraordinaire: Joan Sawyer, Paula Steffan, and Nancy Gardner. My thanks for holding my feet to the fire. I dedicate Chapter 56 to you.

Last, but certainly not least, my heartfelt gratitude goes to my husband, Dan Tenney. Facade would have been a different book without your input and support. I dedicate this book to you.

An Independent Author's Request

I hope you enjoyed Facade. Please help support writers by leaving reviews on the site where you purchased this book. Your comments and reviews are very valuable and I would love to hear your feedback. Thank you, and I hope you're looking forward to Book 3 in the Iris Reid Mystery Series.

Please "like" my Fan Page on Facebook and say hello: https://www.facebook.com/authorsusancory

For early notification of further Iris Reid Mystery Series books, please sign up on my webpage: www.susancory.com

Thanks again!

Susan Cory